Subhadra Sen Gupta has written over forty books for children because she thinks children are the best readers in the world. She loves telling stories woven around history; plotting complicated mysteries and crazy adventures; dreaming up ghostly tales and scripting comic books. In 2014 she was awarded the Bal Sahitya Puraskar by the Sahitya Akademi for her children's books. If you want to start a conversation with her, send her an email here and she promises to reply: subhadrasg@gmail.com.

A Clown for Tenali Rama

Subhadra Sen Gupta

An imprint of Speaking Tiger Books

TALKING CUB
Published by Speaking Tiger Publishing Pvt. Ltd
4381/4, Ansari Road, Daryaganj
New Delhi 110002

First published by Scholastic India (Private) Limited in 2002
This edition published in Talking Cub by Speaking Tiger Books
in paperback in 2020

ISBN: 978-93-90477-16-6
eISBN: 978-93-90477-15-9

10 9 8 7 6 5 4 3 2 1

The moral right of the author has been asserted.

Typeset in Adobe Garamond Pro by Jojy Philip
Printed at Sanat Printers, Kundli

For my favourite teacher and friend,
Narayani Gupta...
Look where your history lectures
have taken me!

chapter one

It was just another Hampi morning; there was nothing special about it. It was an hour after dawn, and Sivakka and her mother were already at work, plucking chillies. These were the small green chillies that give a fiery taste to sambhar and rasam. Sivakka had tied a piece of cloth around her waist, making a small pouch, and walking from bush to bush she plucked the chillies and dropped them in, all the while humming to herself.

Just around the corner, her brother Basava and their father were at work in the family banana grove. This was the best time to get the sweaty outdoor work done—the February air was still cool but once the sun rose it would get very hot. They were using big, sharp, curving knives to cut away the dead leaves and slice off the ripening bunches of sweet, tiny, yellow bananas. Later, the bananas and chillies would be packed and sent to cities like Bangalore and Mysore.

Once in a while, Basava would stop to take a breath, look up to the next hill and think, *this is so boring! I wonder when I can get away and do some carving.* But he knew he would get some time to himself only in the afternoon. In an hour, he and Sivakka would leave for school. They would come home by lunchtime, and only after that would he be free.

In the village of Hampi, you worked in the fields even if you went to school. Their father was a farmer—he had one banana grove, half a dozen coconut palms, a small garden of chillies and two fields (now emerald green with growing rice). He couldn't do all the work alone; the whole family had to help him, and even after working so hard, they barely managed to make ends meet. So when the tourists came— especially during the festivals, and in winter and spring—he and Sivakka would find ways to earn some extra money.

Now the tourists were all over Hampi. You may wonder what there was to see in their small village in Karnataka. But Basava's village was a very special one—there was no other village like it anywhere in the country. You just had to stand at the edge of the banana grove and look around, and you knew.

Hampi stands right next to the River Tungabhadra as the river curves and froths through the hills that surround the village. These hills are not grassy green and full of trees, but bare rock, huge grey and brown-gold boulders piled one on top of another as if a crazy giant had played a mad game with the stones. Below the hills and by the banks of the river, the land was green and beautiful—full of coconut trees, paddy fields, banana groves, and through it, water flowing like shimmering silver in the narrow canals.

Many villages have hills and rivers but in Hampi, among the rocks, in the fields, by the river, and just about everywhere you looked, there were magnificent ruins. Stone temples with tall gopuras reaching for the sky, arcades of shops, palaces, pavilions, lookout points on top of the crags, high gateways...everything was covered with carvings so beautiful it made Basava sigh with happiness.

Prancing horses, grimacing lions, mythical

animals, marching soldiers, dancing women, gods, goddesses, elephants, Nandi bulls, camels… the whole world was carved on the pillars, walls and tall gopura gates of these ruins. For many centuries the world had forgotten about Hampi, but now they were coming back to this magical place. Their little village had become famous again. Hampi was once the fabulous medieval city of Vijayanagar. A city so famed for its beauty that travellers and traders crossed continents, and voyaged the seas to see it.

Once, from the fourteenth to the sixteenth century, Vijayanagar had been the most magnificent city in India, bigger than Delhi, richer than Rome or London. It was ruled by great kings, and the kingdom stretched all over southern India. But Vijayanagar was often at war with its neighbouring kingdoms of Bijapur and Golconda. For over 200 years Vijayanagar was able to keep the Muslim conquerors at bay, but then it lost the war and the great city of Vijayanagar was ruined by the victorious armies. The palaces were burnt, the temples destroyed, the people fled, and slowly the city sank into the countryside, and after five centuries only a small village remained—Hampi.

Basava, who was fourteen, and his twelve-year-old sister Sivakka had grown up among these ruins. People still worshipped at some of the temples, like the Virupaksha and Kodandarama where pilgrims came all year. Now there were many tourists too—foreigners wearing funny clothes, their faces going red in the sun as they wandered about taking photographs. So, like many villagers, Basava and Sivakka too had got into the tourist business. She sold green coconut water and he sold small stone figurines that he and his father carved in their free time.

That day, after lunch, they went to their favourite spot for doing business—it was the hilly path that led to the Kodandarama temple, and beyond it to the Achyut Raya and Vitthala temples. Business was good. Sivakka had sold so many coconuts to thirsty tourists that there was a huge pile of empty coconut shells beside her, and Basava had just sold four carvings to two women from Delhi at a very good price. The local pilgrims would have haggled but these two were not very smart. Basava smiled to himself, trying to imagine his little carvings travelling all the way to Delhi when he himself had never gone beyond Hospet, 12 kilometres away.

Sivakka noticed his satisfied smile. 'The women were nice. The one in glasses gave me this ballpoint pen and a chocolate. You shouldn't have asked for such a high price.'

Basava shrugged, 'Hah! It's business. They knew nothing about the price of carvings. You know, my dancing Ganeshas are selling really well. Tonight, I must carve some more.'

'Well, you do carve them very well; even better than Appa.' Sivakka gave him half the chocolate. 'Eat it up; it's beginning to melt.' Her large dark eyes turned dreamy. 'Basava, do you think Amma would let us go to the dance show tomorrow night?'

Basava shook his head. 'Not a chance! Do you know how much the tickets cost? No one from the village is going. It's really for the tourists. Some of the kids in school were planning to sneak in somehow.'

Sivakka's eyes widened with excitement. 'Sneak in! Do you think we can?'

That night, Basava and his father sat beside the lantern, carving small pieces of granite.

'Sivakka tells me your dancing Ganeshas are selling well. Your carving has really improved, Basava. I like this Nandi bull.'

'I wish someone could teach me to do large figures,' Basava said dreamily. 'Like the Narasimha near the palaces.'

'At one time, the men in our family could make them all—the Krishnas, Narasimha, Lakshmi and Parvatis. They were the royal sculptors of Vijayanagar, but that was 500 years ago; the skill is long forgotten. I don't know how to carve big standing figures, or make the pillars. My father did not have the skill either.'

'Does anyone in Hampi know any more, Appa?' Basava asked curiously, and his father sadly shook his head.

'You will have to teach yourself. Now it is late, go to bed.'

∽∾∾

The next day was a holiday, so the gang of friends met after they had all done their household chores. Their favourite meeting spot was the ruined pavilion that stood in the middle of Basava's father's paddy fields. Hampi was like that—people had 500-year-old carved pillars holding up their cowsheds, put their saris to dry on a palace wall, and pieces of sculpture propped up doors. This pavilion was a small, open, pillared hall and every pillar was alive with carvings. It was one of the loveliest pavilions in Hampi, and sometimes those mad tourists would wade through the paddy field to look at it. Sivakka loved getting photographed by them.

This morning, they had to make urgent plans. That night there was going to be a dance recital at Hampi Bazaar. A famous Kuchipudi dancer was going to perform and they had to find a way to sneak in. There was no question of buying the tickets: they were just too expensive. But a show at Hampi and them missing it? No way!

Venkata, Basava's best friend, scratched a mosquito bite on his thin leg and said, 'There must be some back entrance or something.'

'Sure,' Ratna shrugged, 'and they would leave it wide open for us. Then all Hampi would sneak in.'

'Remember that special puja they had last year at Virupaksha?' Sivakka reminded them. 'We did manage to get in.'

'That was easy—the temple has so many side doors you can always find a way. But this is a pandal, and it is covered from all sides,' Parvati said.

'Let's go and check it out,' said Basava.

Ten minutes later they were wandering about aimlessly in Hampi Bazaar. Even the bazaar was really a ruin. On both sides of a broad road there were rows of open, pillared arcades that were shops once, but now most of them were empty—just small rooms with tilting pillars, collapsing roofs, and weeds growing through the cracks on the floor.

At one end of the bazaar stood the famous Virupaksha temple, the oldest temple in Hampi, and here some of these rooms had become shops again. At the other end stood Matanga Hill. Under it there was a large pavilion that made a perfect stage, and the dance recital was going to be held there. An open pandal had been put up before it, and men were busy setting up rows and rows of chairs.

Trying to look casual, they wandered around the pandal and realized that there were only two entrances: one at the main gate and the other behind the stage. They knew that at the main gate there would be people checking the tickets, so the only possibility was through the back way.

'We'll have to wait here, and the moment we see no one around, we'll creep in,' Venkata said, like a general planning a battle. 'Then crawl to the back behind those chairs and sit on the ground where the guards can't spot us.'

'But before that,' Sivakka grinned, 'we'll have to get out of the house without getting caught. If Amma found out she'd lock us up.'

'Well…I heard the show starts at nine, after the puja at Virupaksha; and usually people at home are asleep by then,' Ratna said optimistically.

ॐॐ

That night, Basava and Sivakka crept out of the house on hearing the soft whistle outside their window. Ratna, Venkata, Viru, Parvati—the whole gang was waiting. They ran through the lanes of the village, up the hill path, and within minutes were at the bazaar. As they ran towards Matanga Hill they could hear the music, and Sivakka gave a despairing wail, 'It's begun already!'

'Nah! Listen carefully; it's all out of tune. They are tuning the instruments.'

They reached the back entrance and then

slid to a halt. The gate was being guarded by two men, and they were turning away anyone without a ticket. It was clear that many people had the same idea as them, and the organizers were ready for them. As they stood there hoping to discover a way to get in, Venkata tiptoed behind the guards and slid inside. But before the others could follow, a rough hand grabbed his shirt as a guard cuffed him hard, making his head ring, and he found himself back with his friends. Later, one guard, spotting them still huddling in one corner, came up menacingly and shooed them away.

'Now what do we do?' Ratna whispered. 'I don't want to just sit here and listen to the music. That is no fun.'

'What can we do? Fly?' asked Parvati, flapping her arms, and then they all looked at their general Venkata, who was surveying the empty ruins of the shops on the two sides of the bazaar with a thoughtful air.

'Is there a way up to the roof?' he asked.

'Yes!' said Viru. 'I know where there is a broken staircase. Let's go!'

In a flash they had run to the middle of the bazaar and clambered up a collapsing stone staircase to the roof of the shops; then, keeping their heads low, they crept towards the pandal. Walking carefully over the broken and tilting stone roof, they got as close as possible without getting spotted, and sat peering over the parapet. If anyone below had looked up, they would have seen a row of small heads but, luckily, no one did. Venkata gave a triumphant laugh, 'This is the best view! We have balcony seats!'

Breathless with excitement, Sivakka looked down at the stage. It was like a dream. The dancer had just made her entrance and was doing an elaborate namaskar. Then she began to dance and Sivakka forgot everything.

This was what she had always dreamed of doing—wearing a shimmering silk sari, her ears, neck and arms glittering with gold and jewels, dancing the Kuchipudi. The dancer's elegant hand gestures, the hasta mudras, her flying feet, the jangle of her anklets, the swaying long braid of hair—she watched it all with great concentration, trying to imprint it on her mind so that she would never forget it.

In her school there was a teacher who had learnt Kuchipudi for a few years, and she had taught Sivakka some of the steps. Her teacher said Sivakka had talent, and she knew the basics like the varnams, the pallavis and tillana, but this dancer was quite special. Sivakka wished she could have been closer to the stage, where she could see the dancer's face better and watch her acting—the abhinaya. Sitting up on the bazaar roof, she couldn't make out the changing expressions on her face that were telling the story that she was dancing to. Sivakka sat utterly entranced by the music, the lights, and the whirling dancer, her head filled with dreams.

Basava was dreaming too, but not of tapping feet and swaying arms. He only thought of stone. He remembered the dancers carved everywhere on the walls of the ruins in Hampi—rows of them, with musicians playing drums and flutes, the flying legs that flared out their saris, the curve of the arms. If Sivakka dreamed of dancing, Basava dreamed of carving a row of dancers on the base of a palace—graceful figures and their beautiful movements, frozen in stone.

Then it was nearly midnight and the stage was empty before them—the show was over. As they wandered home, dreamtime was over too. The chilli garden and banana grove, the cowshed and herd of goats waited for them the next day.

✺

Early next morning, Basava, Venkata, and Viru were at their pavilion. The day before, Basava had noticed that one of the pillars was beginning to tilt rather dangerously; so he had called his friends to help him prop it up. A few months earlier, after the monsoons, another pillar had begun to tilt, and Basava's father had taught them how to save it. What usually happened with the ruins was that, because of rain, the floor of the pavilion would begin to sink and then the pillars would tilt; so if the floor was not fixed on time, the pillar could collapse and take down the roof with it. It had happened to many of the ruins around the village, and the pavilion was too precious. Basava was going to do all he could to save it.

It was hard and sweaty work as they raised the thick and heavy slabs of granite flooring around the base of the pillar. Then they went to a nearby patch of empty land and, carrying back baskets with earth and rubble, began pouring it on the floor to raise its level. Then they would put the granite slabs back on the floor.

As Basava and Viru walked back, staggering slightly under the weight of the heavy baskets on their heads, Viru asked his friend, 'How did your father think of this trick to save the pavilion? It really works much better than using new brick pillars to hold up the roof. Now everybody in the village is doing it to their old buildings.'

'Haven't you seen those men working at the temples? Appa told me they are from the government and they are trained to save ruins. They are putting back the collapsed roof of the Vitthala temple. Appa asked them about the pillar and they showed him how to do it.'

'The government people have even repaired the legs of the Narasimha statue…'

'And dug out that lovely stepped tank near the Mahanavami Dibba. Appa said that they are also teaching the local people to work at the ruins…You know, patch up the cracks, repair the carvings. So he asked them if I could learn, and they have said I can work from next winter, after I have finished my class eight exams.'

Viru grinned. 'You'll like it better than chopping banana plants.'

When they got to the pavilion, Venkata was busy digging a small trench around the pillar where they would add rubble to make the base stronger. Suddenly, his spade hit something metallic with a clang, making him stop to look.

'Oye, Basava, there is something buried here!' He peered down. 'Come here fast!'

The boys crowded around the hole, quickly using their hands to clear the earth around a dirty brown bundle.

'What do you think it is?' Basava wondered.

'A treasure? Gold coins?' asked Venkata the optimist. 'Royal jewellery!'

As they pulled out the bundle, there was another clink inside, making Viru give a breathless, excited laugh. It was a very old leather bag, with a large buckle on top. The leather was cracked and worn, and had turned a dirty greenish-black with age. Venkata pulled impatiently at the strap attached to the rusted buckle, and the whole thing came away in his hand. He upturned and shook the bag, and some rusted pieces of iron fell out.

'Oh!' Viru's sigh was a like a wail of disappointment. 'It's only some iron tools! Who is the idiot who buried it here?'

Basava picked up one piece of iron and studied it closely. 'It looks like the head of a small hammer.' He picked up another. 'This is a chisel. These are sculptors' tools!' he said delighted, as he turned the chisel about. 'It's very well made—see how light it is? It must have been used to carve small figures.' He weighed the chisel in his hand and then said with a satisfied smile, 'This is nice.'

'Nice, hah!' said Venkata, disgusted. 'Here we were thinking of gold coins and you think an old, rusty chisel is nice. You are crazy.' He sighed. 'Oh well, back to work. We have to save our pavilion.'

So, putting aside the bag and its rusty contents, they went back to work. By the end of the morning the pillar looked safe again. As they were heading home for lunch, Basava picked up the bag and Venkata grinned at him. 'What are you going to do with it, my great sculptor friend? Use it to carve your stuff?'

'Maybe. The chisel is still usable, and it is much lighter than the one I am using.'

'But I found it, so it's mine,' Viru teased. 'I'll give it to you for five rupees. Cash.'

'Cash? Forget it! I'll carve you a pretty girl. Will that do?'

'Done!' yelled Viru as he ran towards his home. 'Make her look like a film star!'

⌘

That afternoon Sivakka and Basava were back at work, selling their coconuts and carvings on the Kodandarama road. After laying out the figurines before him, Basava pulled out the old hammer and chisel. He first cleaned off the rust and earth, and then fitted a wooden handle to the old hammer. Then he picked up the rusty chisel and began to clean it, scrubbing it hard with a piece of cloth.

'It looks so old. Won't it break when you use it?' Sivakka asked, leaning over his shoulder.

Basava scrubbed away. 'I don't think so. Appa says that the pavilion has been in our family for many generations. So this chisel must have belonged to some ancestor.' He held it up to check the edge. 'A man who was a stone carver—we've always had them in the family. The edge seems to be quite sharp still.'

Basava picked up the half-done figure of a dancing Ganesha and began to use the old chisel to test it. Sivakka, forgetting to sell her coconuts, leaned against him, watching—she loved to watch her brother carve. There was such a sure touch to the way he would tap softly with the small hammer while moving the chisel over the piece of stone. He would begin with a piece of shapeless granite and after a while, under his hands, it would begin to take shape—a head, arms, legs…

This Ganesha was nearly complete; just the face had to be carved. Sivakka loved the way he would add little touches that made his figures somehow special. A Nandi bull would get a dreamy smile; this Ganesha had a hand curved in a dance mudra and one leg raised in a pose that reminded her of the movement of the dancer they had seen the night before.

One eye was done; now just the second one remained, and then the figure would be complete. As he carefully carved the curving line of the eye, Basava smiled gently at his sister's absorbed face.

'If I had been a sculptor in the time of the great king of Vijayanagar, Krishnadeva Raya, I would have carved this Ganesha ten feet tall and—'

Just as he said this his hands finished the eye, and there was a booming flash. It seemed as if the earth had stopped spinning and was standing still. Suddenly, there was the sound of thunder in their ears. Both of them began to feel dizzy—everything was swaying wildly, and then it went bright and starry. In panic, Basava tried to reach out towards his sister, but he couldn't see because of the stars in his eyes. Their heads began to spin faster and faster, and there were flashes of silver lightning everywhere. Then everything went absolutely dark.

chapter two

Slowly their heads stopped spinning, the light got brighter again, and Basava and Sivakka opened their eyes.

She turned a dazed face towards him. 'What happened to me? Everything went dark for a while.'

'That's what happened to me too! Was it an earthquake?'

They looked around, becoming more and more puzzled. They were still sitting on the Kodandarama road; the hills, the river, and the sky were the same, but everything looked different. For one thing, the people going past were wearing very different sorts of clothes. All the men were in dhotis and lungis; no one wore shirts or trousers. Many were also wearing turbans. A woman went past, holding a round umbrella made like an upturned woven basket;

and all those foreign tourists in hats and dark glasses, and carrying cameras had vanished! And the two women from Delhi who had been nearby, taking photographs of the river, had vanished too!

They stared at each other. Sivakka had been wearing a salwar-kurta, but now she wore the traditional long skirt and blouse; and Basava's shirt and khaki half pants had turned into a short dhoti and tunic.

Then he looked down, and his eyes widened in panic, 'My carvings! Where are my carvings? Siva, I've been robbed!'

'O devaiyya! Where are my coconuts?' Sivakka screamed.

The carvings and coconuts were gone! Basava looked down at his hands and discovered that he was still holding the old hammer and chisel, but that was all they had left. The Ganesha he had carved was gone too. Feeling dazed and shaky they stood up.

'Where are we?' he said. 'This is not our Hampi.'

Basava hid the tools behind some rocks, and then, holding hands, they walked nervously towards Hampi Bazaar. A few minutes later, they stood at the edge of the bazaar and looked around in wide-eyed amazement at a magnificent scene. This definitely was not *their* Hampi!

Instead of the empty rows of ruined shops, the gutters full of smelly water, the wandering goats, cows, and playing children, this was a busy, bustling place. The shops were all spanking new, filled with goods, with shopkeepers calling out to customers. They walked slowly past, peering in curiously—some were full of bolts of silk and cotton, others had gleaming brass pots and pans. One shop was selling only perfumes, and a small open-air arcade was full of fragrant garlands of jasmine and roses swaying in the breeze. Their eyes kept getting bigger and bigger as they saw jewellery shops where gold, pearls, and precious stones were being shown to customers.

By then they had reached the gate of the Virupaksha Temple, where an old woman was distributing leaf plates of payasam to people. At least this had not changed, they thought in relief, as they reached out and got one plate each, and sat eating and looking around. It was like watching a film where they were inside the screen.

'The temple is the same and there is the Matanga hill at the other end of the road.'

'But everything looks so new and rich, and there are so many people.' Then Sivakka made another discovery. 'There are no cars!'

'Where are the tourist buses, and those motorcycles that the hippies ride?'

Instead, there were men riding horses and women getting out of palanquins. Everyone was so well dressed! Even the men wore jewellery, while many women wore silk saris with diamonds twinkling at their ears and noses. They looked very different from the poor farmers and trinket sellers of their village.

Basava was slowly beginning to understand. 'This is another time, an earlier time. Do you think we are dreaming?'

'Dreaming?' She gave him a doubtful stare. 'How can we dream the same thing at the same time? This is some magic that has happened to us.'

'Yes, this has to be magic and we have to find out exactly where we are. But we have to ask very carefully or people may think we are mad.'

'Right! Imagine standing in the middle of a bazaar and asking, "Sir, where are we? What year is it?" They would lock us up for being crazy!'

They had felt quite scared at the start, but after eating the payasam, they were beginning to enjoy themselves. It was such a change from their daily lives, this mad adventure they had somehow got into! And as Sivakka said, as long as they had each other, they would be all right.

They wandered about trying to spot a friendly face, and then Sivakka pulled at Basava's hand. They went up to the flower shop, where a dark, pretty young woman sat alone, threading garlands.

'Akka,' she asked in a small, nervous voice, 'can you help us, please?'

The woman looked up, reached into a box next to her to pick up a betel leaf that she stuffed into her mouth, and then said, 'I don't give money to beggars.'

'No, no,' Sivakka said hurriedly, 'we don't want anything. We just want to ask you something. Please, will you listen to us?'

'Please don't get angry,' Basava said apologetically. 'We have come from a village and we are lost. Could you please tell us where we are?'

The woman looked amused. 'You do talk like village idiots. This is the main bazaar of Vijayanagar, what else? Have you ever seen a grand place like this before?'

Basava shook his head. 'It's really very beautiful.' Then he thought quickly and asked, 'But can you tell us how to reach the palaces? In the village, they said the palaces are very beautiful and we must see them.'

The woman's smile widened, 'They were teasing you. The guards will stop you at the gate. Our king stays there and only the ministers and noble people are allowed to go inside. What do you think—that every villager can enter the palace of our king?'

'King who?' Sivakka tried her best to look very stupid. 'I forget.'

'Tchah! You two really know nothing. King Krishnadeva Raya, who else?'

Next to her, Sivakka heard Basava's soft gasp of delight.

After thanking the flower woman, they came away and looked at each other. Now their eyes were wide with surprise. They knew about Krishnadeva; they had learnt about him in their history lessons in school, and people in Hampi still talked about him. Their magic had taken them back nearly 500 years to the reign of the great king Krishnadeva Raya of Vijayanagar!

Sivakka turned anxiously towards her brother. 'Five hundred years! How will we go back home, Basava?' Basava felt his heart sink a bit too, and he did not have an answer to her question. At least not yet. So to reassure her, he turned an excited face to his sister.

'There must be a way. We just have to find it. Sivakka, imagine! This was the time they were carving the Narasimha statue!' His eyes began shining with real happiness. 'This is what I have dreamed about for years: to see the statue as it was before those soldiers broke its arms and legs. I have to see it before we go back to our Hampi. If we can travel back in time, I'll also work out how to go home. But now we can actually see the great city of Vijayanagar. Oh, Siva! What fun!'

Sivakka was looking at her brother with a doubtful frown.

'Don't you think it is fun?' Basava asked again. 'Imagine travelling back hundreds of years to a time that I have always wanted to see!'

'Sure.' She gave him the look she always

gave when she thought her brother was being especially stupid. 'But we have to eat; we need a place to stay. Amma and Appa haven't travelled with us, remember? And I'm feeling a little hungry again.'

Basava's enthusiasm waned a bit. She did have a point. But then his excitement at being in Vijayanagar returned, and he said optimistically, 'We can always get work. See, there are so many shops, and we can ask that friendly flower girl to help us.'

Still not convinced, Sivakka pointed to the main gopura gate of the Virupaksha temple. 'Shall we go inside? Maybe some other pilgrim will distribute prasadam. I could eat some more payasam.'

The main gopura, the towering gateway of the temple, looked new. Beyond it, the temple courtyard was full of pilgrims. They sat down under a tree and looked around. In some ways, things were different, as they had noticed before—like the clothes—but in others, it was just like their own times. The faces were the same, and the pilgrims were busy with the age-old religious rituals that hadn't changed in thousands of years. One woman had a brass pot with a coconut on top of it balanced on her head, and she was going round the sanctum with a priest chanting mantras walking before her, sprinkling the ground with water. A man was doing elaborate namaskars by lying down full length on the ground. But no one was giving prasadam yet.

'What a pretty woman!' Sivakka said, making Basava turn and follow her gaze. A woman had come out from the inner courtyard where the main shrine was, and now she stood talking to some people. She was tall and slim, and her skin was the colour of pale gold. Her hair, in a long braid, snaked down her back, and Basava's sculptor's eye noticed the large eyes and the perfectly shaped mouth and nose. *She looks a bit like Hema Malini*, he thought. As they watched, she laughed and began walking away, and then to Basava's surprise, Sivakka was streaking across the courtyard towards her.

As the woman walked away, Sivakka had noticed that one of her silver anklets had come off but she had not realized it. She picked it up and went running after the woman, calling, 'Akka! Akka! Oye, beautiful lady!'

The woman turned. Sivakka ran up to her

and held out the anklet. 'You dropped this,' she panted.

'Oh!' The woman smiled. 'Thank you so much. And were you calling me "beautiful lady"?'

Sivakka nodded, trying to get her breath back. 'You are beautiful, and I don't know your name. Now put it on carefully; the clasp must be loose.'

'Quite.' The woman looked amused at Sivakka's bossy suggestion. She sat down on the ledge of a pavilion and began to put on the anklet. By then Basava had joined them, and she looked up at their curious faces, watching her. 'Well, my name is Padmalaya. What's yours?'

'Sivakka, and this is my brother Basava.'

She has such gentle eyes, thought Basava. *Her eyes are like Amma's. Maybe she can help us.* 'We have come to Vijayanagar for the first time...' he began.

'And we are lost.' Sivakka quickly understood what he was up to.

'Lost? You mean you can't find your parents?'

Sivakka shook a doleful head. 'We have no one in Vijayanagar. There is just the two of us, and we don't know what to do, and I am feeling so hungry and scared.'

Padmalaya's eyes softened, 'Oh dear, are your parents dead?'

'They are not in this world,' Basava said carefully. It was sort of correct—they were in Hampi village, five centuries into the future, and at least he hadn't actually killed them off. Sivakka slid a sharp glance in his direction but, to his relief, did not giggle.

'Then you two better come with me. You deserve lunch at least for getting my anklet back.'

They followed Padmalaya to a small house right next to the temple wall. They went to wash up at the small stepped tank next to it, and then the three of them sat down to a simple lunch of rice, sambhar, curd and vegetables. The children were so hungry, they ate silently for a while. Then Sivakka sighed happily, 'Oh, this food is so good.'

Padmalaya smiled. 'It was nice having you two here—I don't really like eating alone.'

'You live alone?'

She nodded, and her eyes were dark with sadness. 'My mother died last month. She was all I had in this world.' She put some more rice on their banana-leaf plates. 'But tell me, if your parents are dead, what are you two doing here?'

'I'm looking for a job,' Basava said. 'We only arrived this morning from the village. Could you help me find something? I am willing to do anything.'

Padmalaya's eyes lingered on Sivakka's soft, rounded face with the huge, liquid dark eyes, and she smiled, 'Well, I do need some help in the house.'

'But I can't cook!' Sivakka protested. 'I can only boil rice.'

Padma laughed. 'I have a cook. You will have to dust and clean the house, wash my clothes, run errands to the market, that sort of thing. You can do it together and stay in the back room in the courtyard. And that would be perfect, because then I won't have to stay alone in the house either.' Then she reached out to caress Sivakka's soft cheeks. 'And call me Akka, I prefer it to "oye beautiful lady".'

Sivakka giggled as she collected the pots and pans to take to clean at the pond.

It was evening, and Basava and Sivakka were sitting outside the house, watching the world go by. A man went past, carrying a basket of vegetables, and it made Sivakka think of home. *Everything feels better when you are not hungry*, Basava thought. Just then, Padma called them, and they went in to discover her standing there wearing an expensive sari, putting on jewellery.

'Help me tie the garland on my braid, Siva,' she said. 'And then give me the jewellery.'

Sivakka bent to her task and asked, 'You are going somewhere?'

'Of course—to the temple. The evening aarti starts in a while.'

'All dressed up like this? Is there a special puja?'

Padma was busy doing up her eyes with kohl. 'Of course not,' she said. 'I am dancing today.'

'Dancing!' Sivakka's eyes widened. 'You dance at the temple, Akka?'

'Of course. Didn't you know? I am the number two dancer at Virupaksha, just after Meenakshi, who is the senior dancer. Today, it is my turn to perform.'

'Oh Akka! How absolutely wonderful!'

Sivakka exclaimed, her eyes shining. 'You're actually a real dancer!'

As Padmalaya laughed at the little girl's delight, Basava thought that now his sister wouldn't be so unhappy about staying a while in Vijayanagar. *One day, well go back to our own Hampi*, he thought, *but not yet. I have to see the Narasimha statue first.*

Next morning, they woke to the sound of conches being blown at the Virupaksha Temple to welcome the new day. Then came the rising chant of melodious mantras and the ringing of bells. They could smell the incense that filled the air.

Basava and Sivakka sat up. 'We're still in Vijayanagar!' he said, looking around, grinning at his sister. 'I thought we'd wake up at home.'

'Oooh Basava!' Sivakka smiled. 'Do you remember Padmalaya's dance last night? Wasn't she wonderful?' Then she said bossily, 'We have to start work. Get up!'

While Padma went for puja to the temple, they spent the morning doing the kind of household chores they did at home anyway.

Sivakka swept the courtyard and rooms, and drew kolam designs on the threshold with rice powder. Then she washed the clothes, had a bath, and helped the cook, grinding the spices and making breakfast. Basava chopped up some firewood, carried in water from the river, and then went to the market to buy fresh vegetables.

Padma made them sit with her at breakfast and asked a lot of questions about their lives—where they came from, what their father did. They made up a story, which was sort of similar to their own lives, but when she asked how their parents had died, their voices faltered and they were silent. To their relief, the soft-hearted Padma did not persist with her questions.

Later in the morning, as they sat on the veranda—Padma folding betel leaves, putting lime paste and cardamom on them; Sivakka busy threading jasmine garlands for her hair—a shrill, feminine voice called from the lane.

'Padmalaya, are you home?'

'Oh no!' Padma sighed. 'Not first thing in the morning.'

The woman walking towards them wore a bright crimson silk sari covered in gold embroidery and she had such a lot of jewellery on her that Sivakka wondered how she managed to walk. There were huge circular earrings, a heavy gold necklace, bangles, armlets on her upper arms, diamonds on her nose, rings, and anklets. As she came jingling towards them, Basava studied her face. Once, she must have been beautiful, but now she had grown rather plump, and the red paan-stained lips and angry frown did not help. In contrast, Padma, with her freshly washed hair, wearing a simple cotton sari and little jewellery, looked much more beautiful.

Padma stood up and did a polite namaskar, and they followed. The woman, ignoring their greetings, said roughly, 'I want to talk to you about last night. You've been up to your tricks again, Padma!'

'Last night? What tricks?' Padma looked puzzled.

'Why did you dance to that padam? You know I was planning to use it tonight. Now I have to change my programme again! Padma, why do you keep spying on me?'

Padma's smile vanished. 'Spy? Don't be ridiculous. That padam was chosen by the wife of Minister Saluva Timma when she came to do puja yesterday. If you don't believe me, you can ask her maid. Also, I don't know and don't care what you plan to dance tonight.'

The fat woman, who was all ready for a fight, was stopped by Padma's words. She glared at them, her face flushed with rage. Then, muttering something rude under her breath, she wheeled around and strode away.

'Aiyo! Who was that?' The kids turned to Padma.

'That is my daily headache.' Padma gave a helpless shrug. 'She is Meenakshi, the leading dancer at the temple. She starts a fight with me twice a week.'

'Why? What have you done to her?'

'Nothing. Meenakshi was once a great dancer but now she's become fat and lazy and doesn't practice enough. So when my dancing is praised, she gets jealous and comes to fight. That's why I want to leave.'

'Leave?' Sivakka's eyes widened. 'Where will you go?'

Padma grinned. 'Down the road. The new Krishna temple that the king has built is nearly complete. I want to become the chief dancer there—but don't tell anyone, because I know Meenakshi will try to spoil my plans.'

'How?'

'She wants to be chief dancer at both temples, and she has the support of Raghunath, who is the Head Priest of Virupaksha.'

'Then what do you plan to do?'

'I have to find a way to dance on the inauguration night of the temple—the pratishthanam ceremony. I'll dance so well people will forget about Meenakshi…'

'And her fat legs,' said Basava, and they all laughed.

However, the argument with Meenakshi must have upset Padmalaya, and she wandered about the house with a glum face. So when they heard her greet someone with a happy laugh, they came out to look. A dark, stocky man wearing a dhoti, short tunic and turban stood in the main room talking to Padma. She called them closer, saying, 'Kartikeyan, these are the children helping me in the house. They work very hard.'

Kartikeyan studied them and then said, 'Get them some new clothes, and,' he turned to Basava, 'I hope you don't mind helping me a little? I need someone to carry some bundles to the temple site.'

'Of course not. Which temple?'

Kartikeyan looked quizzically at him, 'The Vitthala, where else?'

'Oh, they don't know,' Padma said hurriedly. 'Kartik works at the site of the new Vitthala temple being built by our king.'

'Are you a stone carver, Kartikeyan?' Basava asked optimistically.

Kartikeyan gave a crooked grin. 'You can say that. Actually, I am the Chief Sculptor at the site. I am designing all the sculptures in the temple.'

Basava gave a small jump of delight. 'First class! Kya baat hai!' He had picked the phrase from a Hindi film.

'What was that?' Kartikeyan turned to stare at Basava. 'What did you say?'

'Oh nothing, just something I heard,' Basava hurriedly changed the subject. 'What do I have to carry?'

A few minutes later, Basava, laden with a bundle of mats and an earthen pot of lunch packed by Padma, followed Kartikeyan, who was striding ahead carrying his toolbox. He tried to talk, and discovered that Kartik was a man who did not like making polite conversation; so they walked on in a companionable silence. Basava looked around, comparing the place with his Hampi. They had taken the road by the river and there were many more huts on the way, though these looked as small and poor as the ones in his village. People sat weaving baskets and a potter was at his wheel. *Vijayanagar had many more people than Hampi*, Basava thought, *but ordinary people weren't any richer than in his time.*

Then they reached the site of the new temple and Basava was in heaven. Everywhere, large chunks of granite lay on the ground, most of them cut to the length of pillars and panels, and the carvers were at work on them. Rows of men bent over the stone, and all you could hear was the sound of hammers and the chink of chisels, and the air was full of stone dust. He wandered about in a daze of happiness, watching a man carve the fantastic shape of the prancing lion-like creature called a yali, with a man riding it. Another was doing an intricate border of flowers and leaves; a third was busy finishing the face of a goddess. This was Basava's world!

An excited Basava ran to Kartik, who was checking the work of a carver, a middle-aged man working on a long panel, and asked anxiously, 'Kartikeyan Anna, can I work here please? I know a little carving and I want to learn.' The men looked at him with amusement. 'You don't have to pay me anything,' Basava continued. 'Just let me learn from you.'

'No,' said Kartikeyan, and walked away.

Noticing his disappointed face, the other carver said kindly, 'Don't mind our Kartik—he is not a very polite man. He doesn't have the time to teach you, but if you want you can sit and watch me, and if you are any good, I'll let you help. My name is Chinappa.'

'And I'm Basava, and thank you so much, sir! I can't tell you how grateful I am. You see, all my life I've wanted to carve stone.' He stroked a chisel lovingly. 'This is all I have ever wanted to do.'

'Then get to work, boy,' said Chinappa shortly.

And in this way Basava found himself a teacher.

chapter three

N ext morning, the children were very busy. Sivakka followed Padma everywhere like an adoring puppy, and Basava was shadowing Kartikeyan. Padma was amused and patient with the girl, while Kartik ignored the boy. The night before, while going to bed, Sivakka had wondered when they could go home. She was feeling homesick again. She missed her parents a lot—they must be so very worried, looking for their lost children everywhere. Then there was this family wedding coming up and her dress wasn't ready. Sivakka cried a little before falling asleep; but in the morning, with the bright sun outside her window and Padma singing in the next room, she had forgotten her worries.

However, there was a niggling little thought running through Basava's head—he didn't really know how they had travelled back in time, so when they wanted to go home, what would he have to do? He had hidden his problem from Sivakka but he was becoming more and more worried. But once day broke and Kartik arrived, he had other things to think about. An incorrigible optimist, he thought, *I'll work it out when we decide to go back. I'm not going back yet. I have much to learn from Chinappa and Kartik.*

Leaving Sivakka absorbed in watching Padma at her morning dance practice, he followed Kartikeyan to the temple site, carrying his bag of lunch and tools. On the way, he again tried to talk. Not that Kartik encouraged it.

'Kartik Anna, how did you learn to carve stone?'

'From my father.'

'Padma said you have created a new kind of pillar design. Will you show it to me please?'

'You can see them yourself. I am carving one now.'

Devaiyya! Basava sighed, *give me patience, what's wrong with this man? Does talking make his stomach ache or what?* But he persisted, 'Would you mind if I watched you at work?' Kartik turned to look at him, so he added hurriedly, 'I'm not asking you to teach me anything.'

'Fine, but stay quiet.'

Ah well, maybe one day he'll talk to me, thought Basava, *maybe he'll even smile.* He wondered how Padma liked Kartik so much.

At the temple site, Basava strolled around happily, watching all the stone carvers at work. Then he settled down next to his friend Chinappa, who said, 'Right now I'm carving this apsara's face and I have to concentrate. So sit quietly and I'll teach you later.'

'What'll happen if I talk?' Basava asked cheekily.

'My chisel may slip and the apsara could go cross-eyed or get a flat nose. Then Kartik will dance the tandava on my head.'

Basava sat back and looked around, thinking, *I'm the only one here who knows how the temple will ultimately look.* Now it was only half built—the main temple's natyamandapam, the hall before the sanctum where the dancers performed, was nearly complete. The rest was a confusion of blocks of stone and bricks. *I wish I could tell Kartik that five centuries later they will say that his temple was the most beautiful in Hampi.*

Then he remembered with sadness that it was also in ruins—the gopura gateways were broken, the roof of the natyamandapam lay in pieces, and the inner sanctum where the idol of the god, Lord Vitthala, should have been standing, was dark and empty. No one came to worship any more at Kartik's temple. And though those government people were working to restore it, the temple was too badly damaged to be fully repaired. He knew the temple could never be complete again.

Chinappa looked up. 'Why are you looking so glum? Has Kartik been rude to you?'

'Not really. It's just that he seems so angry all the time.'

'That's just his way of speaking—ignore it. He doesn't have much patience and always speaks his mind, but he is good at heart. He is the best Chief Sculptor I have ever worked with; he's a little mad, like all talented people.'

'But there is a lot of anger…'

Chinappa sat back and took a pinch of snuff. 'He is the most talented sculptor in Vijayanagar but he hasn't received the credit he deserves. I wish he would learn to be a little tactful; speak politely to the noblemen and ministers. Instead, he is rude to them. Fortunately, our king discovered his talent, or our Kartik would still be carving pillars.' He picked up his chisel. 'Come here, let's see what you can do.'

Basava began his first lesson and time flew. There were so many tricks of carving that Chinappa knew—the best angle at which to hold a chisel to carve different kinds of surfaces, how to use the hammer, when to hit hard, when to tap, and it was such fun working on a large piece of stone. As Chinappa watched, he carefully carved a border of flowers and leaves. The old man nodded, 'You do have a carver's hands but there is a lot to learn. You'll work on this pillar with me.'

'Kartik won't mind?' Basava asked anxiously.

'He's the one who suggested it. But get a smaller chisel and hammer; my tools are too heavy for you.' He smiled gently at Basava's shining face. 'There is nothing that feels as good as carving stone, is there?'

Speechless, Basava just smiled back.

&

In the evening, Basava was again walking back with Kartik, carrying his things. However, instead of going towards Kartik's house behind the bazaar, they walked on.

'Where are we going?' Basava asked a bit nervously.

'To the Krishna temple. I want to show you something.'

The temple was past a hump in the hill, and beyond the old temples on Hemkutam hill. Basava remembered that just a short walk beyond it was the giant Narasimha statue that he wanted to see. So he said carefully, 'Is there a Narasimha statue, too, nearby?'

Kartik looked puzzled. 'No. There are two Ganeshas and the big Nandi bull in the bazaar.' He turned to stare. 'Where did you hear of a Narasimha?'

'Oh!' Basava was quiet for a moment and then said, 'I must have heard wrong.'

Obviously, the statue was not built yet. He would have to be more careful about what he said or he could get caught. He had to warn Sivakka about it too—she never thought before speaking.

They entered the newly built Krishna temple. Some people were still at work, giving finishing touches. The ceilings were being painted in many jewel-like colours; the pillars were painted white.

Kartik walked up to one of the outer pillars and said, 'This is the design Padma was talking about. What do you think?'

Basava studied it critically. Here, instead of a solid block with carved sides, the pillar had been divided into a circle of slender columns in the middle, making it look light and elegant. 'It is good here, but you have improved it at the new temple.'

Kartik looked interested. 'So you notice the difference?' Basava nodded. 'Chinappa did say you pick things very fast.'

He reached out to touch a pillar. 'At this temple I was just one of the carvers and no one took me very seriously when I created this design. The Chief Sculptor even made changes which ruined the design, but I could not say anything.' He smiled slightly at the boy listening so intently. 'You think I am a very angry man, don't you? That is why I feel so angry. Many of the best ideas here are mine but all the credit will go to the Chief Sculptor, a fool who couldn't design a bathhouse, forget a temple. All he knows is how to copy others.'

'Your design is much better at Vitthala, much better balanced.'

'I want Vitthala to be the most beautiful temple in Vijayanagar.' They began to walk back towards the bazaar and Basava smiled in the darkness at the dreamy note in Kartik's voice. 'I owe it to our king. He came to the temple site one day and immediately noticed that I was doing something different in my work, and he gave me this opportunity. I will not let him down. Krishnadeva Raya's Vitthala Temple will be the wonder of the city. Just you wait and see.'

And then he laughed. Basava joined in, feeling tempted to tell Kartikeyan that, yes, his temple would be the wonder of not just the city but the world, and people would travel from across the seas to see it. Kartikeyan's magnificent dream would live for centuries.

After dropping Kartikeyan at his house, Basava headed for the hill road to the Kodandarama temple. He wanted to collect the hammer and chisel that he had hidden there. He clambered up the rock just above where he and Sivakka had been sitting, reached down in a hollow and with a sigh of relief pulled out the tools. Basava had a feeling he'd need this ancient hammer and chisel to go back to modern Hampi, though he hadn't a clue as to how to use them. He just knew in his heart that the hammer and chisel had a magic in them.

He sat back and looked around—from that height he had a panoramic view of Vijayanagar. Night had fallen, and everywhere the oil lamps had been lit. He could see the flickering golden flames in the huts by the river and in the houses built on the slope of the hills. Around the temples, palaces, and the bazaar, it was blazing with the light of torches. Just then he heard a commotion, and turned his head to the sound of yelling and running feet coming from the direction of the Kodandarama temple.

In the shadowy light, he could vaguely make out people running, and as they got closer, it looked like one man was being chased by a group of men. The man in front, running at a furious speed, suddenly swerved to hide behind a boulder lying on the side of the road, and then very stealthily began to climb the rock face. He clambered up close to where Basava was sitting, looked up and noticed the boy. A hissed whisper said, 'Don't tell them I'm here! Or they'll kill me!' The head disappeared again.

Basava looked down—the men who had been chasing were now standing right below him. They looked like brahmin priests, in white clothes, with their head shaved in front, the long hair knotted at the back, and sandalwood marks on their forehead. One of them looked up and spotted him, and yelled, 'Hey boy! A man came running here, did you see him?' Basava nodded. 'Where did he go?'

Basava pointed to a steep, narrow track that led down to the river and watched the men gallop away in the darkness. Then, very slowly, the head reappeared from behind a rock and a nervous whisper asked, 'Are they gone?'

'Yes. I sent them down to the river.'

'Oh, bless you, boy. May Lord Virupaksha make you a rich man! That was very clever! You're really a quick thinker, I must say.'

By then, Basava and the man had climbed down and were walking quickly towards the bazaar. In the light of the shops, he turned to survey the man he had saved. He was a tall, thin fellow wearing a dhoti, with a shawl wrapped over his chest, and he seemed to be holding something under it. The face was long, with hollow cheeks, round comical eyes, and a sharp beaky nose. He looked surprisingly calm and cheerful for someone who had just been chased by men waving thick sticks. He bowed his head and gave a crooked grin. 'Malappa at your service. In me, you now have a friend for life.'

'Thank you.' Basava was a bit doubtful if he wanted the man as a friend but still, one had to be polite. 'I'm Basava. Tell me, why were the men chasing you?'

'Oh, I stole their bag of coins,' Malappa said casually, and pulled it out from under the shawl to show him.

'Stole it?' Basava's eyes widened. He had never met anyone who actually admitted to stealing before, even when they were caught red-handed.

'They are priests at the Kodandarama, and at this time every evening, they count the money the pilgrims leave in the hundi box and carry it home. So I snatched the bag.'

'You are a burglar?'

Malappa gave a toothy grin. 'The best! No one has caught me yet.'

'I noticed you ran really fast. You could have won the 100 metres at the Olympics.'

'Won where?'

'Oh nothing,' Basava said quickly. 'Just a race I had heard about.'

He was finding it oddly difficult to dislike this friendly, cheerful burglar. By then they had reached the main bazaar. To Basava's surprise, Malappa strolled up to the garland shop and greeted the woman who had chatted with them on their first day at Vijayanagar. They seemed to be great friends; and while chewing one of her paans, Malappa gave her a detailed account of how Basava had saved him.

The woman shook her head. 'When will you stop stealing, Malappa, you fool? There are so many other ways to earn a living!'

'Give up? Not while I can run and my legs are holding up. This boy says I could win a famous race.'

'Well, as long as you steal, I won't marry you—that is certain.'

'Oh really, Manjira, it's a good profession! We've been burglars for generations—it's our family trade.'

Manjira glared at him; Malappa grinned.

Leaving the two still arguing away happily, Basava headed for Padma's house and discovered Sivakka standing anxiously at the door. So, to calm her down, he had to tell her how he got so late. Sitting down to eat dinner with Padma and his sister, he wondered at how quickly he was getting used to this life, meeting new people, making friends. *If only Amma and Appa had been with us*, he thought moodily, *we would have never gone back to Hampi. Appa and I would have become sculptors, Siva could learn to dance...*

Later that night, the three of them sat in the courtyard. Padmalaya was telling them of her life. She was the daughter of a temple dancer, and from her birth, it was fixed that she would follow in her mother's footsteps. She was a devadasi and, like the other dancers, she was married to the god of the temple, Lord Virupaksha. Sometimes she wished she could leave the temple and marry, but that was not allowed. She would have to remain a temple dancer all her life.

'That means you can't marry Kartik Anna?' Sivakka asked.

Padma smiled. 'I am married to Lord Virupaksha. Even if Kartik and I decide to defy everyone and marry, and if I had a daughter, she would have to dance too. I don't like my life being chosen by others, especially by men who do not understand.'

'But couldn't you dance in other cities? Sell tickets for your performance.' Basava's business brain was working quickly. 'You know, dance on stage, in films…' And then he stopped—he'd dropped another brick!

'Who'll pay to see me dance, when you can see dances free at temples? And what is this umm…filim?'

'Uh…a sort of dancing play I had heard about,' Basava said a bit lamely.

'You two talk very strangely sometimes,' Padma said with a puzzled smile. 'This morning, Siva was talking about travelling by a flying chariot.'

'I forgot, Basava,' Sivakka said in a small, apologetic voice. 'I just thought I heard a plane and ran out to look.'

'She imagines things,' Basava said, trying to cover up for his sister, and then quickly changed the subject. 'But Padma Akka, maybe one day there will be flying chariots…'

'And boxes in your houses that play music or show pictures.'

'And lamps you don't have to light with oil.'

Padma stood up with a laugh, ruffled their hair, and said, 'Sure. And I'll dance on the moon.

You two really should become storytellers. Now go to bed.'

Next morning, when Kartik and Basava reached the temple site, they were told that King Krishnadeva Raya was coming to see the work in progress at his new temple. Basava sat next to Chinappa, breathless with excitement, watching the royal guards arrive first and stand at attention at the gate, holding swords. Then the king's personal gold palanquin was carried in, followed by other royal men, nobles, and ministers, who came riding on horses.

Basava looked wide-eyed at the man his school history textbooks described as one of the greatest kings of India. Krishnadeva was much taller than most of the men surrounding him, and his dark, slender body had the broad shoulders and strong arms of a warrior. He wore a simple white dhoti with a gold border, a plain tunic on top, and a deep blue silk uttariya draped over his shoulders like a shawl. All his jewellery—a necklace, bangles, rings, earrings—was made of gold, set with precious stones, and his long hair was tied in a knot at the back. He moved quickly, and his eyes did not miss anything as he walked up to study every new bit of carving. He carried himself with an easy majesty, and there was often a smile on his sharp-featured face. *He looks kind*, thought Basava, *but also tough. I wouldn't disobey him easily.*

'Who are all those men with the king?' he asked Chinappa.

'That man who is talking to the king is Tenali Rama. He is the court poet, and a friend and counsellor of the king.' Basava saw a short, lively looking man who would be remembered by children five centuries later for his clever words and funny tales. It was obvious Tenali liked talking.

'That white-haired old man,' continued Chinappa, 'is Saluva Timma, the king's Chief Minister. He helped our king to the throne, and is the most powerful man in the kingdom. That young man behind him is his son Timma Dandanayaka.'

Saluva Timma? The name sounded familiar. Basava tried to remember what he had learnt about him in school. He had also read some books about Krishnadeva, and there was something in them about Timma and his son that he couldn't remember—something that had made him angry. But he couldn't ask Chinappa either, because maybe the shocking thing hadn't happened yet.

Kartikeyan, as Chief Sculptor, and the man who was the temple architect took the king and his entourage around the temple site. All the other workers stood at a distance, and when the king went past, they kept their heads bowed, because you did not look the king straight in the eye. The architect showed him the plans of the temple. Kartik pulled out drawings of the new designs of pillars that he was doing. Listening to them, Basava realized that the king understood the finer points of sculpture and was making some good suggestions. All the while, Basava was trying to remember the story of Timma and his son, but it had vanished from his head. Then the king gave money as rewards for the carvings that he had liked, and Chinappa went up to get a bag of coins for his carving of the apsara. Basava was about to begin clapping, and then stopped himself just in time!

The king had left with his entourage, but Tenali Rama had stayed back, happily wandering about, chatting to the carvers. Watching him, Basava thought of all the funny Tenali stories he had heard since he was a child, of how he could fool everyone and make the king laugh. As he sat practicing carving a lion's head and a Ganesha's face on a stray piece of stone, Tenali wandered up and perched himself nearby, watching him. Basava dipped his head in greeting, but went on working.

'Aren't you a bit young to carve stone?' Tenali asked. 'He is learning, sir,' Chinappa spoke up quickly. 'Kartikeyan feels the boy has talent, so I am teaching him to carve.'

Tenali studied the Ganesha. 'Your god has a nice smile, I see.'

Basava looked up, pleased that someone had noticed. 'Anybody who gets so many sweets to eat will smile,' he grinned. 'I make my Shivas very serious.'

'Oh, and why is that?'

'Imagine having a son like Ganesha with the appetite of an elephant! It must be expensive to feed him.'

Tenali began to laugh. 'Ah, a carver with a sense of humour. Now this I like! How about doing a funny carving for me?'

'A funny carving?' Basava asked, quite puzzled at the request. 'How can a carving make you laugh, sir?'

'Think about it. If it is good, there will be a prize for you.'

৵৽৾

Meanwhile, Sivakka was bored. Padma had gone off to the bazaar. As she had nothing to do, she wandered out of the house. Just as she turned the corner of the lane, she heard the sound of the mridangam—someone was dancing! She crept upto the open window of a house and peered in. Inside, Meenakshi was rehearsing with a group of musicians—a man with the drums, a singer, and a flute player.

Fascinated, Sivakka stood still, watching as the singer began reciting the beat of the dance and Meenakshi's feet moved in perfect synchrony. Then he began to sing a padam about Lord Krishna, and Meenakshi began to enact the age-old story of the baby Krishna getting caught by his mother, stealing butter.

Sivakka realized that, for all her bad temper, Meenakshi was a very good dancer. Instead of a fat woman, she had at that moment really become a small boy. Her abhinaya was perfect and so was her dancing in the quick passages like the tillana, though she was panting and sweating a lot all through.

Sivakka was so absorbed in watching, she stood up and leaned against the window sill to get a better look. That was when Meenakshi saw her. She stopped dancing, pointed to the window, and screamed, 'Catch that girl! She is spying!' Before Sivakka could run, one of the maids had come out and caught her. She was dragged into the room, where Meenakshi held her roughly by the arm and slapped her.

'I know this girl. She works for Padma. Didn't I tell you, Raghunath, that she spies on me?'

A middle-aged man, who looked like a priest, had been watching the dance. He now frowned at Sivakka's tearful face and said, 'Tell us truthfully—what were you doing here?'

'I wasn't spying!' Sivakka protested fiercely. 'Why should I? I only looked in when I heard the mridangam. I didn't even know she stayed here.'

'Padma didn't send you here?'

'Of course not! Padma Akka doesn't even know where I am, and she dances much better than her anyway,' she said looking at Meenakshi, 'She's too fat to dance.'

Raghunath laughed. The musicians hid their smiles, making Meenakshi furious. As she raised her arm to slap her again, Sivakka butted her in the stomach with her head, making the dancer lose her balance. In a flash, she was out of the house and streaking home.

When she got home, Padma was coming down the lane. Sivakka ran to her and said breathlessly, 'Akka, I think I've got into trouble.'

'You think?' Padma's eyebrows shot up. 'What did you do?'

'I was watching that fat one dance and she caught me. So I butted her in the stomach and…' The whole story came out in a confused, tearful rush.

Padma began to laugh. 'Well, it is trouble alright. Meenakshi won't let me forget it, but I think I can handle it. Just stay away from Meenakshi and Raghunath from now on. He is the Head Priest and Meenakshi's friend, and he doesn't like me.' As Sivakka nodded, she added, 'And to keep you away from trouble, you start dance lessons with me this evening.'

Sivakka's face bloomed with happiness.

chapter four

That evening, with an audience of Basava and Kartikeyan, Sivakka began her first lesson with Padmalaya. First, she and Padma did a small puja to Lord Virupaksha, who in his form as Nataraja is the lord of dance; then Padma tied the bells around her ankles and Sivakka dipped down to touch Padma's feet. Basava knew exactly how his sister was feeling— he had felt the same mix of nervousness and excitement when Chinappa had put the hammer and chisel in his hand with a small muttered prayer to Lord Vitthala. *There is no feeling as wonderful*, he thought, *as learning an art that you love, whatever it may be—singing, dancing, weaving, painting or carving stone…*

Kartikeyan sat leaning against a wooden pillar in the room, watching Padma and Sivakka dance. Sivakka bent and stretched her body, tentatively following the beat of Padma's feet, curved her arms and tried to create images with her fingers. Then Padma, repeating the beat aloud, would dance some more, showing her how to do it right. Basava, sitting at Kartik's side, noticed how absorbed he was in watching Padma. *Looking at Kartik, you would think he was watching an apsara dance*, he thought, amused. And Padma knew it too, because once in a while she would whirl past Kartik with a naughty grin, flicking her long braid of hair at his face, making Sivakka giggle.

After a while, Basava began to feel a bit bored, and drifting out of the house, strolled towards the bazaar. Dusk was falling over Vijayanagar; the temple bells began to ring, calling the devotees to the evening aarti at Virupaksha. There was the smell of incense in the breeze; also the sound of horses' hooves, the call of shopkeepers and vendors. At a food shop, vadas were being fried in hot, hissing oil; in another, milk was being boiled to make sweets, and in a huge pan of sugar syrup, jalebis were circling in delicious twists. Then, as he got closer to Manjira's stall, he could smell the roses and jasmines. Basava took a long, happy sniff and thought, *Our Hampi bazaar doesn't smell so good; it's mostly smoke and cow dung now, and petrol fumes from the tourist buses.*

Manjira was a popular lady, and she was surrounded by a knot of admiring men. Basava had noticed earlier that the women moved about freely everywhere in Vijayanagar, and many shops had women serving the customers. He used to think that in ancient times women always stayed at home or were in purdah. It obviously was not true of Vijayanagar. Manjira was sitting there chewing paan and chatting with a group of men. Basava spotted Malappa, the friendly burglar, among them. Basava went up to listen to the men talk.

One man, a soldier, had just returned to Vijayanagar after a military expedition, and he was telling them about his adventures. The fortress of Raichur was claimed by both Vijayanagar and the kingdom of Bijapur. It had been occupied by Bijapuri soldiers; so Krishnadeva Raya decided to capture it. He took a huge army of seven hundred thousand soldiers, seven hundred elephants, many horses and cannons, and laid siege to the fort. Inside were the men of Ismail Adil Shah, the Nawab of Bijapur, who came quickly to rescue his men, and there was a fierce battle near the Krishna river.

The Nawab, a very clever man, had hidden cannons behind the army lines, and when the Vijayanagar forces drove into the Bijapur army, these guns opened fire and the horsemen of Bijapur followed right behind. There was panic, and for a moment it looked like Vijayanagar would lose. But then Krishnadeva rode out in front, facing the guns himself, and led his army into a counter-attack that took his soldiers straight into the Bijapur camp. Ismail Adil Shah fled to save his life and his army was scattered. Vijayanagar laid siege on the fortress and won Raichur.

Malappa shook his head in admiration. 'Our king is truly unbelievable. He always leads the army himself. Most kings let their commanders do that, but not our Krishnadeva Raya!'

'That is why Vijayanagar has never been defeated after he became king.'

'And it is not easy being king of Vijayanagar,' the soldier said. 'We are surrounded by enemy kingdoms—Bijapur, Golconda, the Gajapati of Orissa...'

Listening to their excited voices, Basava remembered Hampi as it was 500 years later and his heart filled with sorrow. *One day, this great kingdom would be defeated*, he thought, *and I can't tell them that because they would never believe me.* After Krishnadeva Raya, Vijayanagar would be ruled by weak men who would fight with each other and fail to defend the kingdom. Then, one day, the armies of Bijapur and Golconda would come sweeping in, and take out their bitterness of two centuries of defeat by turning this beautiful city into a ruin.

He thought of the smashed carvings, the palaces that had nothing left of their wooden halls, the traces of fire on the ceilings of the temples, the marks of hammer blows on the statues, and his heart ached. War is always terrible, even though men boast and talk about it as if it was something to be proud of. Someone always paid the price of war, and it was usually the innocent. Poor people died, great cities were destroyed, children were orphaned…The ruins of Hampi told you how cruel war could be for people.

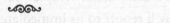

The men had left; only Malappa remained. Suddenly, he gave a yelp of panic and said, 'Oh devaiyya! I better hide!' As Manjira and Basava watched in astonishment, he bent low and crawled into the shop, and vanished behind a pile of garlands.

Basava turned to see four priests walking purpose-fully down the bazaar towards the shop.

'The priests from Kodandarama! They are coming this way!' hissed Manjira. 'Don't say a word!' As the men came up to the shop, she smiled sweetly and held out a garland. 'Flowers for the noble lords?'

'We want to talk to you,' one man said bossily, ignoring the offer of flowers. 'A man has been seen at your shop: a tall, thin, ugly fellow with a hooked nose...'

'Many men come to my shop—it is very difficult to remember,' Manjira said politely. 'But why are you looking for him? And what is his name?'

'We don't know who he is, but he has stolen our money—the sacred *hundi* money from the Kodandarama temple. So if you see him you will report to us immediately.'

'Of course!' Manjira smiled. They watched the men walk down the road and turn the corner towards the temple.

'Are they gone?' Malappa whispered, still hidden from view. As Manjira nodded, he breathed, 'Oh thank you, Manjira! You saved my life, and you are a queen among the garland girls of Vijayanagar.'

'Forget the flattery. Next time I won't save you—that's a promise, you ugly burglar!'

Malappa's head slowly rose from behind the flowers, his round eyes now like saucers in indignant protest. 'Ugly! How dare the priest call me ugly! He looks like a bad-tempered buffalo himself.' Then he sat up and said thoughtfully, 'Do you think I should grow a moustache? Then they wouldn't be able to recognize me…What?'

He stopped in surprise and stared at Manjira and Basava, who were doubled over with laughter at the sight of Malappa sitting with a bunch of roses balanced on top of his head and a jasmine garland dangling over one ear.

'Oh Malappa, they were wrong!' Manjira giggled. 'You're the prettiest burglar in all Vijayanagar!'

Next morning, as Chinappa and Kartikeyan were busy, Basava had no carving lessons. Padma had gone shopping, so Sivakka was free. So they decided to go sightseeing. They wandered out of the Vitthala temple, and through the long stretch of road where a bazaar would come up once the temple was completed. All the temples had a connecting bazaar like that, where during the chariot festival, the idol of the god was taken out in a procession in a huge wooden chariot.

They walked past houses and fields, orchards and flower gardens, under a huge gateway, and came to the banks of the Tungabhadra river. It was the Telarigattu Ghat, the main landing stage of the city. In Basava's time, it was a small, ramshackle ghat from where you took boats to cross the river, but here it was a big, busy place with huge boats flying sails, piled high with goods, waiting to unload by a long stretch of steps. The place was noisy with boatmen, workmen and traders.

'Look, Basava!' Sivakka said. 'The boats haven't changed at all.'

The round coracle boats were exactly like the ones they used at Hampi to cross the river to reach the Anegundi fort on the other side. As the boatmen took you across, the boats went round more than forward.

Padma had given them some money to spend, and with it they bought some spicy fried stuff from a food shop and sat watching the scene. All the while, Basava was thinking about what Tenali Rama had said to him: 'Carve me something funny.' He thought about all the kinds of carvings he had seen at the Vitthala—nobody was doing anything that could be called 'funny'. *What was a funny carving anyway*, he brooded. *I'm sure Tenali was teasing me.* Absently, he took a stick and began to draw in the dust. What he drew was the funniest thing he had seen in Vijayanagar: it was Malappa the burglar's long, thin, cheerful face.

After he had drawn Malappa's face, Basava remembered how he had looked with the roses on top of his head and the garland dangling over one ear—just like the clowns he had seen at the circus at Hospet. So he gave Malappa a tall cap with a bell, and then he was drawing faster—a rattle in one hand, a funny, dancing pose. He bent the clown's legs in opposite directions at the knees, and added odd pointy shoes.

Basava stood up. 'Let's go back to Vitthala, Siva. I have a carving to do.'

At the temple site, Basava found a small flat piece of stone and some charcoal sticks. He began to draw what he had dreamt up at the ghat. Then, with a small prayer, he began carving the outline of the figure. By afternoon, the shape of the clown was much clearer, though it would take Basava some days to carve it fully, when he would add the finishing touches of the hooked nose and the round eyes. He wondered if he should show it to Chinappa and Kartik; but then he thought they liked doing dancers and lions, riders and goddesses, and they would not find a clown amusing.

Basava was so absorbed in his work, he hadn't realized that someone had come up to stand behind him. Then a voice said, 'You are truly a clever boy. How did you know what I wanted?' Basava looked up to see Tenali Rama's smiling face.

'That is a very funny carving. It makes me think of myself,' he said with a laugh.

'Actually, I wasn't thinking of you when I drew it,' Basava said seriously.

'No?' Tenali's dancing eyes widened, his

eyebrows rose. 'I'm disappointed. You mean there's a man in Vijayanagar who looks funnier than me?'

Basava began to smile. 'He is a burglar.'

Tenali Rama laughed out so loudly, some of the carvers working nearby turned to look. 'A burglar! Really Basava, this is truly a disaster! The handsome and famous Tenali Rama beaten by a burglar!'

Suddenly, Basava remembered that he was talking to one of the king's trusted advisers and not just a kind man.

'I didn't mean to be rude, sir…' he began.

'I understand,' Tenali said gently, 'and I enjoy the way you talk to me as a friend, not always being courteous.' He pointed to the carving. 'I like that jester you're carving because that is one of my jobs—making the king laugh.'

'Why do you have to do that?'

'Because Krishnadeva has a very tough life, full of work and worries. We all forget that he became king when he was barely twenty, and since then he has had the burden of running this kingdom on his shoulders. Then, we are surrounded by enemies and he spends months at the battlefields. He needs me to make him forget the worries, add a bit of laughter to his life.'

'People never forget your jokes. They'll remember them for hundreds of years.'

'Well, hundreds of years sounds very optimistic, but if I am remembered as someone who helped Krishnadeva in any way, that would be enough.' He leaned back against a half-done pillar and continued, 'Sometimes you can say a lot through a funny anecdote. Most people don't take me seriously because I joke and laugh, but the king knows that at times I give advice that way.'

'How do you do that?' Basava asked, puzzled.

'Once, the rains failed and the astrologers were called. They said the rain god Indra was angry and he would only be appeased by a sacrifice. And that the next day, the soldiers should go out and capture the first living creature that was asleep facing the south. This could be an animal or a human being and it had to be sacrificed during the yajna.'

'Then what happened?' Basava asked breathlessly.

There was a slight smile on Tenali's face, as if the memory of that time still amused him. 'Next morning, when the soldiers came out of the palace, the first thing they saw was me and my pet dog lying on the palace steps, facing the south!'

'Oh!' Basava breathed.

'The soldiers were very confused but they took me and my dog to the king. Then I asked the astrologers, "Now, whom will you sacrifice? This dog named Appu or this dog named Tenali?" Everyone looked at the king, who began to laugh, and said, "No one will be sacrificed. We will only have the prayers."'

'He understood what you were saying,' Basava smiled.

'Yes, that taking a life cannot be auspicious. And then—would you believe it—the same afternoon it began to pour. Appu and I went out and danced in the rain.'

Tenali and Basava laughed happily together.

'His Highness trusts you,' Basava said admiringly.

'Yes. He can't trust too many people. It can be very lonely being a king.'

Again, Basava remembered the disquiet he had felt watching Saluva Timma. He spoke very carefully, 'That old man with the king—can he be trusted?'

'Minister Timma? Of course! He is like a father and adviser to the king. He helped Krishnadeva win the throne, and the king trusts him with his life.'

'I thought his son Timma Dandanayaka had a very cruel face…' Basava gulped. 'Oh! I shouldn't have said that, pardon me!'

Tenali shrugged, 'Ah well, you have a point there. Saluva Timma has spoiled his son, and the boy is not intelligent like his father.' He looked thoughtfully at Basava. 'You notice a lot, don't you? Also, unlike most subjects of the king, you talk very freely.'

That is because I am from another, freer time, thought Basava, amused. He said, 'I should be more careful, I suppose.'

'Not with me. I like hearing what you say.'

Just then, Kartik came up, followed by Chinappa and Sivakka, curious about what Tenali was doing for so long with Basava. Meeting Tenali, Sivakka's eyes shone. 'Oh sir, I have heard all your stories and I love them all! And my friend Ratna always says she would have loved to meet you and tell you some of her favourite jokes. There is one she heard on the radio—' Sivakka's eyes widened as she came to a ragged halt. 'I mean she heard from a friend...'

Tenali looked a bit puzzled, 'You have a friend called what? Radio?'

'No, no, sir...' Basava quickly came to his sister's rescue. 'This friend is called Radha but they tease her and call her Radio.'

'Yes!' said Sivakka in relief.

'Radio, radio...' Tenali brooded. 'I like the sound of it. I think I'll call my cow that. What do you think? A cow called Radio? Nice, what?' He gave a satisfied smile, watching the two children giggling so hard they had tears in their eyes. Then he turned to Kartik and said, 'Actually, I came to meet you, Kartikeyan, but these two little monkeys distracted me. I remembered your request for the dancer Padmalaya and spoke to Queen Tirumale Devi, and she has agreed to see her dance. If Her Majesty likes the performance, Padmalaya can dance on the inauguration night, at the pratishthanam ceremony of the Krishna temple. Tell her to come to the queen's palace tomorrow evening.'

Next evening, a very nervous group of people got off a bullock cart driven by Kartik at the main gate that led to the palaces of Vijayanagar. First came Padma all shimmering in silk, then Sivakka carrying a basket of flowers, then Basava holding tight to a bundle that held Padma's jewellery, and then the musicians. It was the time for Padmalaya's audition before Queen Tirumale Devi.

As the performance was to be in the women's quarters, Kartik was not allowed in. Even the musicians had to play from behind a screen. Basava, luckily, was still considered a boy and was let in by the palace guards. A guard took them down a long road running beside the high wall surrounding the king's palaces. They came to a fork in the road and turned to the left towards the queen's palaces. To the right was the king's enclosure with the new temple that the king had built for his personal use, called the Hazara Rama temple because it had many carvings on the life of Lord Rama.

The queen's palaces were hidden behind high walls, with watchtowers that had women guards. Inside, there was a large compound with many palaces, pavilions, pools for bathing, gardens, and shady trees. The place was busy and noisy, with many women lazing beside the pools. Some chattering maids went past, carrying clothes and pots for washing. The queens, princesses, and other women of the royal harem sat at the windows, or on swings under the trees. One woman was busy feeding her parrot; another sat painting under a neem tree.

Basava, who had often visited the ruins of what is now called the Zenana enclosure at Hampi, immediately noticed the main large palace. In his Hampi, all that remained was the carved stone base; here he saw the brick and wood building that had stood on it. It had delicately carved wooden pillars, brick walls around large halls, filled with beautiful furniture, sculptures in metal, painted walls and ceilings.

They were led into a smaller palace, the prettiest in the place—one that still stood in Basava's time and was called the Lotus Mahal. It was painted a pinkish yellow colour and had beautiful arched doorways. A maid, waiting for them at the door, took them inside and told Padma to get ready. The queen would come after the evening puja. Padma put on the flowers and jewellery, the musicians tuned their instruments, the singer cleared his throat, and Sivakka nervously chewed her nails.

Basava looked around and thought, *Ah, so this is how these palaces looked inside.* In his Hampi, they were just empty halls. Here, the floors were covered with thick carpets. Tall metal oil lamps stood in the corners. The walls were hung with rich tapestry, and there were low divans and small tables everywhere. Flower garlands swayed over the doorways, and bowls of fragrant roses and jasmines were placed around the room. Soft bolsters were strewn around for people to lean on, and the air was softly perfumed by incense smoke rising lazily from bowls.

When Queen Tirumale Devi entered, they all bowed low with folded hands. Sivakka looked up and held her breath. Krishnadeva Raya had also come to watch Padma dance! The royal couple settled down against a pile of bolsters, and the king, with a wave of his hand, asked Padma to begin. Sivakka said a small prayer to Lord Virupaksha and then forgot everything as she drowned in the magic of Padmalaya's performance.

Padma had decided to dance what she enjoyed the most: a soft, romantic number that told the story of Lord Krishna and Radha, and then a fast tillana that showed her talent in pure movement and rhythm. So, first there was graceful abhinaya, showing her power of acting, and then scintillating passages of lightning-quick dance movements that dazzled the eyes. And tonight, Padmalaya was dancing for something she wanted, so she danced with her heart.

Basava, whose interest in dance never lasted for very long, let his mind wander. Here, in the more intimate surrounding of a personal room, he could look up and watch Krishnadeva and his queen. The king looked tired and a bit absent-minded, and Basava remembered how Padma had told them that he was rather a sad and worried man because he had no son and heir. Though he had two queens, none of his sons had lived, and he was growing old; he needed an heir to take over the kingdom. And then, finally, Basava remembered what he had read about Saluva Timma and his son, and he sat frozen in shock.

One day, Krishnadeva and Tirumale Devi

would have a son and they would name him Tirumaladeva. The king would abdicate in favour of the young prince. Tirumaladeva would become the king, with Krishnadeva acting as regent to make sure that no one snatches the throne away. But the boy would die of poisoning and the main suspect would be Timma Dandanayaka, Saluva Timma's son. In the beginning, the king would refuse to believe this—for him Saluva was like a father, a man he trusted and loved. In the end, however, he would blind and imprison Saluva and his two sons, and the old man would die in prison. Krishnadeva would end his days a sad and bitter man, and he would be succeeded not by his son, but by his incompetent younger brother Achyut Raya.

I don't like this, Basava thought, *this knowledge that I have of what will happen in the future. I hate it. No one will believe me if I speak up in warning, and even if I did, it won't change anything; all this has already happened. It is just this burden in my mind. I hate this. I want to go back to Hampi.* He suddenly realized he had tears in his eyes and bent down to wipe them at the edge of his dhoti. Basava suddenly felt very old, and he couldn't bear to look at the faces of the king and his beautiful queen. *It is unfair*, he thought, *that such a great and generous man would have to face such grief.*

By then, Padma had come to the end of her performance and stood anxiously waiting for the queen's verdict. Krishnadeva smiled at his queen and said, 'The temple is for you, so it's your decision.'

Tirumale Devi smiled back. 'Then, Your Majesty, I do want Padmalaya for the Krishna temple ceremony. I have seen her dance before and I know that she dances with true devotion.' She took off two of her gold bangles and gave them to Padma, saying, 'I will be sending you the clothes and jewellery to wear at the performance. Padmalaya, you must not let me down.'

In a daze of excitement, they came out of the palace gates and saw Kartik waiting for them. One look at their shining faces told him the good news, and it was a very happy and excited bunch that went chattering home. In all the talk and plans, the laughter and teasing, no one noticed that Basava was rather quiet. Basava's heart was heavy and he was finding it difficult to feel happy about Padma. In the Lotus Mahal he had come to a decision: very soon it would be time for him and Sivakka to go back to Hampi. It was just that he had to first find out the way to go back. What was the magic? What did he have to do?

The cart came to a stop at Padma's door. As they were getting down, Sivakka glanced towards the temple and saw Meenakshi and the head priest Raghunath standing there, watching them. There was something in the way they stood that made her nervous. Kartik saw them too and grinned at Padma.

'It looks like the news of your success has already reached your friends. They don't look very pleased.'

Padma, still floating in happiness, just laughed, but Sivakka was worried.

That night, Basava had fallen asleep but woke at the sound of someone crying. He lit the lamp to find Sivakka sitting up in bed, sniffing morosely.

'I miss Amma!' she wailed. 'At night, I hate sleeping alone. I want Amma...'

'Do you want to go back to Hampi?'

Sivakka swallowed. 'Yes! It is fun here, but not without Amma and Appa. Can we go back in a few days, please, Basava? Once you have learnt some more about carving and I have had a few more lessons with Padma?'

'Yes. It will probably take a few days to discover how to go back, but I think it is time to start planning.' Basava reached into his tool bag, pulled out the magic hammer and chisel and said, 'You know, I have been thinking. I think I will have to carve a dancing Ganesha with this like last time, because I have used these to carve other things and nothing happens. So the magic probably only works with a Ganesha. Only, when I am carving it, you stay close to me. I don't want to go back to Hampi and find I have left you behind.'

'Then you will have to carve at night in this room. When no one is around.'

'I'll get a piece of stone tomorrow.'

chapter five

Next morning, Kartikeyan and Basava were about to leave for the Vitthala temple when they stopped at the door at the sight of Raghunath and Meenakshi marching towards Padma's house, followed by two hefty men. Nearing the door, Meenakshi began to yell for Padma. Sivakka and Padma, who were in the kitchen, came rushing out hearing all the noise.

'Raghunath has something to tell you.' Meenakshi had a triumphant glitter in her eyes that made Sivakka's heart sink.

Raghunath came forward with an important air, and said, 'Padmalaya, is it true that you went for an audition to the palace last night?'

'Yes. Everyone knows that.' Padma looked puzzled.

'Without my permission?' Raghunath's chest

swelled with indignation. 'I am the head priest of the Virupaksha temple!'

'When the queen of this kingdom invites you,' Padma smiled slightly, 'I don't need anyone's permission. And before you ask, Her Majesty Queen Tirumale Devi has chosen me to dance at the pratishthanam ceremony at the Krishna temple. And if I'm good, I become the Chief Dancer there.'

'That means nothing!' Meenakshi said disdainfully. 'Only the king can appoint a Chief Dancer. I danced before King Vira Narasimha, and it was he who chose me for this temple.'

Kartikeyan, who had been watching things quietly so far, began to laugh. 'Sorry to disappoint you, Meenakshi, but the king was there too and he agreed with his wife. Now, are there any more questions or can we go back to our work?'

Raghunath was clever enough to realize that it would not be a good idea to anger Padma and Kartik now that they were in favour with the king. He gave a cold, polite smile. 'Congratulations to you—but then, Padmalaya, you will kindly vacate this house today. I cannot allow the worship of Lord Virupaksha to suffer and will have to appoint another dancer immediately in your place, and she will need a house.'

'And take these brats with you,' Meenakshi added spitefully.

'What do you mean?' Kartik leaned forward threateningly. 'This is her house, Raghunath. Now you stay away…'

But Padma reached out to hold him back. 'No, Kartik. He is right; this house belongs to the temple and is given to a dancer. So I will have to leave.'

'But where will we go?' Sivakka's eyes widened with worry.

'We'll find a place in the bazaar, till the Krishna temple can find me a house.'

'Good. Try to leave by the evening.' Raghunath turned to go. 'I don't want to use my men to throw your things out on the road.'

'Well, if your men are willing to pick up the luggage, will they carry Padma's things to her new house instead? We'll pay them good wages,' Kartik asked very politely, though his eyes danced with laughter. 'They look like good strong men.'

As the four of them began to laugh, Meenakshi and her entourage walked away, glaring angrily back at them.

As Padma, Sivakka, and the cook got busy packing, Kartik and Basava went hunting for a house. It took them all morning because Kartik was so very hard to please. One house was too far from the river; another too near the bazaar, a third didn't have a courtyard...

'If you don't make up your mind fast, Kartik Anna,' Basava sighed, 'we'll end up sleeping out in the open tonight.'

Finally, one house got Kartik's approval—a small two-roomed house, in a quiet corner near the new bazaar coming up for the Krishna temple. It had a wide porch, a courtyard with a huge tree, and a well. By afternoon, all Padma's things had been shifted in, and she looked around with an excited laugh. 'Oh Kartik, I like this house!'

'And it is quite close to my home,' Kartik grinned back.

'I'm hungry!' Sivakka protested. 'Can we discuss the house later? I just checked—there is nothing cooked in the kitchen either.'

So, big earthen pots of hot rice, sambhar,

vegetable fries, upuma, pickles, and round amritis were brought from a nearby food shop, and as Sivakka said, she didn't mind shifting everyday if the food was so good.

~ew~

Having arrived at the Vitthala temple late, Kartik and Basava were still at work when all the other carvers left in the evening. As Basava sat beside him finishing the clown, Kartik critically studied the crazily dancing figure, and said, 'I hear Tenali likes this jester?'

Basava nodded, grinning.

Kartik continued, 'He would. He has an imagination that's wilder than yours.' Kartik bent over the rearing yali, a mythical lion he was carving, softly chipping away at the stone to create the lion-like mane. 'Oddly, Chinappa likes it too. He asked me if he and you could carve some jesters on the pillars…'

'Can we?' Basava asked a bit nervously.

'Well, I don't like them, but you two are free to do so. I prefer Narasimhas and…'

'Apsaras that look like Padma Akka!' Basava said cheekily.

'Watch it! I'm your guru, remember?'

'Yes, sir!'

Quietly happy, they worked on side by side. Basava discovered that Kartik had a different way of teaching from Chinappa. While the latter would talk and scold all the time, often sitting beside him and guiding his hand, Kartik was much more easygoing. He said little, but his eyes missed nothing, and once in a while he would point to a patch of carving and then show Basava how it was done better. As he said, each carver has to create his own way of working, there were no rules in creating things.

Basava, feeling a bit tired, laid down his tools and looked around the deserted temple, silent after the day-long noise of hammers hitting chisels. 'They will say for years, when you are in Vijayanagar, go and see Kartikeyan's great Vitthala temple.'

'No, they won't.' Kartik sat back. 'They will say Krishnadeva Raya's great Vitthala temple. I would be long forgotten. No one remembers the men who actually build these temples and palaces or do the carvings and paintings.'

'Of course they'll remember you!' Basava said hotly.

Kartik shook his head with a smile. 'Do you

know who built Virupaksha or the temples on Hemkutam Hill?' Basava shook his head. 'I don't either, and the style of carving that is unique to Vijayanagar really begins there. Once, I went around checking every pillar, hoping some carver had chiselled his name somewhere, but I found none. The carvers, painters, architects... we're always forgotten; only the names of the kings live on.'

'Do you mind that?'

'Not really. What does it matter once I'm dead? As long as the king lets me work on stone, I don't need anything more. My carvings will stand and the king can take the credit.' He looked around. 'You are too young to understand, but for me carving is not only a way to make a living, it's also the way I worship Vitthala. Padma dances her prayers; I carve mine. And when you say a prayer, you don't put your name on it.'

'I do,' said Basava promptly. 'I say, please kind Lord Virupaksha, this is your servant Basava's special prayer. Listen very carefully and I'll give you a prasad of twenty bananas.'

'Quite. You're a practical businessman who would have no problems striking a bargain with god.' Kartik reached out to ruffle Basava's stone dust-covered hair. Then they gathered their tools in the bags and got up to head for home.

As they turned into the main road, they saw Sivakka come hurrying towards them, looking rather excited. As she ran up to them, Kartik asked anxiously, 'What's the matter, Siva? Any problems at home?'

She shook her head. 'Padma Akka sent me to call you because Manjira, the garland seller from the market has come to see us.' She skipped along, trying to keep up with Kartik's long strides and continued a bit breathlessly, 'And she said she heard Meenakshi boasting that she has a new plan to ruin Akka.'

'Ruin Akka? What do you mean?'

'She says Meenakshi is planning to spoil Padma Akka's performance on the inauguration night of the temple!'

When Kartik, Sivakka and Basava got to Padma's house, they discovered Manjira and Malappa waiting for them. Basava was rather pleased to see his favourite burglar in Vijayanagar, and wondered if he should tell Malappa that he was now the model for a carving of a clown. But first they had to listen to the latest news.

Manjira had quite a story to tell. That morning she had gone to Virupaksha with a basket of garlands to sell to the pilgrims. She was sitting near Raghunath's room and she immediately knew something was up when she saw him and Meenakshi coming from somewhere, looking upset and excited.

'They were returning after throwing me out,' Padma said with a grim smile. 'They should have looked very pleased with themselves.'

When Raghunath and Meenakshi went inside, Manjira crept up closer to the door to listen. It seemed Meenakshi was furious with Raghunath as she had wanted Padma to be insulted and thrown out immediately, with her things being dumped on the road. Instead, he had spoken politely and given Padma time to find a house.

'Aiyo! Did the two quarrel! She was screaming so much, all the monkeys ran away.' Manjira was laughing so hard she could hardly talk. She took a deep breath and continued, 'That was when she said that she did not trust him anymore and would do things herself. And he laughed, saying she could do nothing to stop Padma, now that the queen was Padma's patron.'

'And what did she say?' Sivakka leaned forward eagerly.

'She said she would make sure that Padma did not dance on the inauguration night,' Manjira ended triumphantly.

There was a thoughtful silence. Then Malappa said, 'That doesn't help much. How can she stop Padma? Couldn't you find out some more?'

'Of course I did!' Manjira said disdainfully. 'You think I'd give up so quickly? Padma is an old friend; we've grown up on the same lane. I wasn't going to let her down.'

When Meenakshi stormed out of the temple, Manjira picked up her basket and followed. Reaching her house, Meenakshi sat down on the porch to pant and fume; so Manjira settled down beside her, looking very sympathetic. She offered her some paan, got a hand fan, and began fanning her; all the time making soothing noises. When Meenakshi had calmed down, Manjira asked what the matter was and heard a long list of complaints against Padma.

'And I nodded and agreed with all she said.' Manjira rolled her eyes at Padma. 'And even said some nasty things about you.'

'Go on!' Malappa said impatiently. 'Stop stretching the yarn.'

With a glare at him, Manjira continued. She said Meenakshi then spoke to her maid, saying that some people would be coming for dinner that night. Then she laughed and said, 'And after tonight we'll see how Padma dances at the pratishthanam ceremony.'

Kartik looked puzzled. 'But that doesn't tell us what she plans to do.'

'Of course not!' Malappa said impatiently. 'We'll have to find out when they meet and get plotting tonight.'

'How? We're not invited to dinner,' Kartik grinned.

'You forget,' Malappa tapped his chest, 'I'm a burglar. So tonight I'll sneak into a house to listen and not steal.'

'What a grand idea! You are just great!' Basava's eyes gleamed. 'Please, Malappa, can I come too? I've always wanted to see how you break into a house.'

'Do you have burglary experience?' Malappa asked quite seriously. Basava shook his head. 'Then I can't risk it. But you can wait for me outside the house and warn me if you hear anyone coming.'

It was night. Malappa and Basava had reached Meenakshi's house and stood across the lane, under a tree. Malappa looked around and said, 'You sit behind the tree and keep an eye on the lane. If you hear or see anything suspicious, imitate the call of an owl to warn me. If you get scared, go home; but whatever you do, don't try to follow me inside.'

Then, as Basava watched, Malappa seemed to melt into the shadowy light of the moon. He crossed the lane like a ghost, slid quickly past the gate of Meenakshi's house, and suddenly, he had vanished! Basava settled back against the tree trunk and waited. A little later, he saw Raghunath and another man come briskly down the lane. Meenakshi opened the door and by the light of the lamp she was holding, he caught a glimpse of the mysterious man's face. He looked familiar, but Basava couldn't remember where he had seen him before. Then, all was quiet except for an odd bark from the street dogs or the tap of a night-watchman's stick. Basava yawned and wished he could also steal into the house, but remembered Malappa's warning.

Basava had dozed off when a huge hullabaloo made him sit up in panic. Malappa was racing out of the house. 'Run!' he yelled, and the two of them bolted down the lane, followed by two men shouting, 'Catch! Thief!' at the top of their voices. Then, a watchman also joined the chase.

Again, Basava marvelled at how fast Malappa could run. His long, thin legs moved at lightning speed as they streaked up the Hemkutam hill. They ran behind Virupaksha, up the slope, in and out of the temples, and then he swerved sharply to enter a dark, deserted pavilion right at the top and skidded to a halt. Panting hard, they moved deeper into the dark interior. Far away, they could hear the shouts, but Basava realized they weren't getting any closer.

'They won't come here,' Malappa panted. 'We're safe.'

'Why not?'

'Monkeys. The hill temples are full of them, and they hate being disturbed at night. So those men can't search for us.'

'Won't the monkeys attack us?'

'Not if we stay here quietly till dawn. So find a place and go to sleep.' Basava saw a gleam of teeth in the dark and there was a smile in Malappa's voice. 'Don't worry, I've hidden here before, so the monkeys know me.'

It took a while for his heart to stop thudding. Basava could not remember when he fell asleep—it had been a very eventful day—but when he woke, the sky outside was becoming light. He looked around a bit dazedly and then remembered the happenings of the night. A snore told him Malappa was still asleep. He came out of the pavilion and the sight before him made him catch his breath in delight.

Dawn was breaking over Vijayanagar. To the east, the sky was turning from a greyish pink to a deeper orange, and the shadowy shapes around him slowly became clearer. A cool breeze began to blow, and the tall spire of Virupaksha's gopura to his right and down, the slope of the hill before him, the shadowy silhouettes of the temples and pavilions slowly appeared out of the gloom. Then, the first rays of the sun caught their spires and gopuras and turned the stone to a beautiful red-gold against the blue of the sky.

Far away, he could see the silvery gleam of the Tungabhadra River, and the green of gardens and orchards, the areca and palm trees reaching towards the sky. And in the smoky haze of the dawn, the boulder-strewn hills all around stood out starkly against the landscape, like sentinels standing guard over the city.

As he sat watching dreamily, the light brightened, and slowly Vijaynagar woke to the new day. The temple bells began to ring and he seemed to catch a whiff of incense from the homam fires in the air. The smoke from cooking fires rose lazily from the houses below. People began to move out onto the streets, and then he heard Malappa wake.

He came out yawning and scratching his head, and said, 'Let's move before our friend Raghunath comes looking. And all that running has made me really hungry. I could eat a dozen idlis.'

Trust a burglar to spoil the mood, thought Basava, amused, as the two of them headed down the hill towards Padma's house. He began to walk faster; Sivakka would be worried, and he was dying to hear Malappa's story.

When Basava and Malappa reached Padma's

house, they were welcomed by two anxious faces at the door. It looked like neither Padma nor Sivakka had slept much the night before. As they listened breathlessly, Malappa had quite a story to tell.

After leaving Basava outside Meenakshi's house, he had stealthily entered the courtyard, and discovering a pile of baskets in a corner, promptly hid behind them. A little later, some people arrived and Meenakshi and her maid got busy serving dinner. Then the maid went off to her room and Meenakshi entered the sitting room with a tray of paan.

'Aha! I thought, now they will start plotting,' Malappa continued his tale. 'So I slipped across the courtyard and stood behind a pillar close to the door to listen. It was a risky thing to do but I thought this was too...'

'Oh really, Malappa!' Sivakka said impatiently. 'Tell us what you heard; we'll listen to your thoughts later.'

'This one is sharp like a green chilli,' Malappa grinned and tapped Sivakka on the head. 'And bossy too. Well, to go on with the action, there were two men who were Meenakshi's guests—Raghunath and a mridangam player...'

'Of course!' Basava sat up. 'That's where I had seen him! I thought he looked familiar. He played for Padma Akka at the temple and also in the palace.'

'Ramaiyya?' Padma asked startled.

'Yes, that's what they called him. He was told by Raghunath and Meenakshi that he was to agree to play for you, rehearse with you, and then on the night of the performance, he was to feign illness and not go. So you'd be left stranded without a drummer and no time to find one either. Then they gave him a bag of coins to keep him happy.'

'Oh! I could kill someone,' Padma fumed. 'How could Ramaiyya do this to me?'

'He didn't want to, but the two bullied him and threatened that he would get no work at Virupaksha if he played for you. And think of him—he is a poor man. The temple is the biggest in Vijayanagar, and he gets regular work there. Ramaiyya can't afford to defy Raghunath.'

'Fine. Then I'll find someone else. There is no shortage of mridangam players here,' Padma smiled at Malappa. 'And thank god you heard their plans. I don't know how to thank you for all you have done for me.'

'Just drop a good word about me in your friend Manjira's ear,' he grinned, and then getting up, took a step, clutched at one leg and groaned.

'You are hurt!' Basava leaned forward anxiously. 'You are limping so badly.'

'I must have twisted my leg while running up the hill—this ankle is all swollen. That Raghunath can really run fast and I was worried he would recognize me. First, the priests at Kodandarama, and now Raghunath. It looks like all the temple priests of the city are searching for me. Life would get really difficult this way.' He took another step and groaned even louder.

'You stay right here,' Padma said. 'I'm not letting you go till you can walk. I'll make some ointment for the ankle. Basava, run to the garland shop and tell Manjira that Malappa is here, and that he has hurt himself.'

Basava groaned, 'But I am hungry! What about some idlis first?'

ॐ

They were still eating breakfast when Manjira and Kartik arrived together and heard a report of their adventures of the night before. All the while, Malappa groaned and tried to look very sorry for himself.

'Serves you right,' Manjira said tartly. 'Burglars always get hurt.'

'Oh really, Manjira, this time he was helping me,' Padma protested as she put an ointment of turmeric on Malappa's ankle and bandaged it.

'But how did you get caught?' Kartik asked curiously 'Basava says you two were chased up the Hemkutam hill. I thought you were such a master at hiding, you could turn yourself into a ghost and vanish like the mist.'

'Go on, laugh at me,' Malappa said morosely. 'You don't know what a chase we had last night. They were inches away from us, and if that watchmen had caught us, he would have beaten us black and blue with his stick.'

'Who saw you?' Sivakka wanted to know. 'I thought they were all inside, busy talking.'

'Well, little chilli, there I was standing behind the pillar listening to them talk, and I was so busy listening, I forgot about that old maid who had gone to her room. She came out and saw me, and as she was behind me, I didn't spot her.'

'I thought you had eyes behind your head,' Basava teased.

'Very funny. Suddenly, this old woman started screaming at the top of her voice and I nearly died of shock. Even then I would have got away, because I had managed to get to the door, but then that fat dancer saw me...'

'And did we run!' Basava laughed. 'And it was the monkeys that really saved us.'

'I came to a decision last night,' Malappa said. 'I'm giving up burglary. It's just too much trouble. My legs are giving up, and if Meenakshi could spot me so fast, then I am losing my touch. It is time to retire.' He gave a sidelong glance at Manjira, 'And then maybe one garland girl will look kindly at me.'

'You mean it?' Manjira's eyes shone. 'You are not joking again, are you?'

'I am buying a shop on the new market road of the Krishna temple.'

'Selling what?' Sivakka wanted to know.

'Vegetables—including little green chillies that are hot like you and make people jump.'

There was a knock on the door and Kartik went to see. He came back carrying a large brass salver covered with a piece of silk. 'The

messenger said, the queen has sent this for you.'
He handed the salver to Padma.

Under the cloth there was a red silk sari covered with delicate gold embroidery and some gold jewellery: a beautiful necklace made of tiny mango-shaped gold motifs, a pair of bangles with pearls set in them, and a pendant to put in the parting of the hair. Queen Tirumale Devi wanted her chosen dancer to look truly gorgeous and regal on pratishthanam night.

Later in the morning, Padmalaya and Sivakka went looking for a mridangam player. Padma needed a drummer immediately, because she had to start rehearsing with him. She was planning a very elaborate dance recital with some very complicated numbers, and she had been depending on Ramaiyya playing for her because he knew how she danced. But now she had to find another man and get him to play right.

First, they tried the other drummers who played at Virupaksha, but it was clear that Raghunath had already got to them—they all made excuses and refused. There were many other temples, and Padma and Sivakka visited two of them but no one was willing to play for her. The sun was high in the sky; Sivakka was beginning to feel tired and hungry as they trudged homewards.

'Now what will you do, Padma Akka?' she frowned anxiously. 'Couldn't Kartik Anna play for you instead?'

For the first time in hours, Padma smiled. 'Kartik has no sense of music or talas. If he played, the soldiers would arrest him for disturbing the peace.'

chapter six

In the evening, when Kartik and Basava returned from the temple site, the first thing they asked was whether Padma had found a mridangam player. Padma's stormy face gave them the answer.

'Don't worry,' said Kartik soothingly. 'There is still time. We'll find one.'

'What do you mean there is time? There are just two days left!' Padma glared angrily at him. 'I need at least one day to rehearse with a new drummer so that he understands what I plan to do. Siva and I spent all day looking for a drummer, and all you can say is don't worry; and then you go off to hammer your stone.' Padma marched out of the room and banged the door behind her.

'Kartik Anna, you better do something; this

is getting serious,' Sivakka said solemnly. 'She didn't eat any lunch either.'

Kartik nodded. 'Tomorrow is "look for mridangam player" day, Basava. No hammering of stone, or you and I can say goodbye to lunch.'

As Padma had not eaten anything all day, that night Kartik cooked dinner, with two nervous assistants in Sivakka and Basava. The cook was sent home and Kartik got busy preparing what he called his 'famous' menu. First, mosaru anna—a delicious mix of curd, rice and spices. Then, with plain rice, there was the soupy lentil of rasam, followed by soppu pallya (a tasty steamed spinach dish), thayir vade (vadas in curd), and a light kosumbari salad. Then for dessert, Basava hurried to the market and got laddus and jalebis. It was quite a spread and, as Sivakka said, except for the fact that the chef forgot to add salt to the rasam, the meal was just great. And their messy efforts in the kitchen finally made Padma smile.

As they were going to spend the next day hunting for a drummer, Kartik decided to get some work done that night. He had brought along some of his drawings, and sitting on Padma's porch with a tall oil lamp, he brooded over them late into the night. Basava sat watching, absorbed in the way Kartik's hand moved swiftly over the paper as he developed a design, marvelling at the new ideas, and the way he slowly created a completely new figure or motif for carving. Most of the carvers he knew just followed what they had been taught by their fathers, but Kartik thought in new ways. He was creating a standing figure of a dvarapal—a doorkeeper—a tall figure of a man wearing an unusual turban and playing a drum.

'It's beautiful!' he breathed softly. 'He looks so real.'

Kartik rolled up the drawing and then said, 'That one was easy, but there is one design that I do not know how to make.'

'What design?'

Kartik unrolled another sheet, and Basava saw that it was the floor plan of the temple. By the light of the lamp they bent over it.

'This is the architect's plan,' explained Kartik. 'And I have to decide where I want to place the sculpture.' He pointed to the different buildings in the plan. 'In the centre is the main temple with the natya mandapam in front, where the dancers will perform. Here is the sanctum where the idol of Vitthala will be placed. Here is the kalyana mandapam, where every year they will celebrate the marriage ceremony of the god and goddess. Here are the other pavilions: the bhajana mandapam, where they will have the singing of hymns; this is the kitchen; and this is the hundred-pillared hall for other ceremonies. And all around it, the pillared corridor and the three gates with the tall towers of the gopuras.' He turned to look at Basava, 'What do you think?'

Basava looked puzzled. 'Think? What is there to think? This is the usual plan of all temples— it is no different from Virupaksha. What makes it different is the fine carvings you are doing and the detail of the designs.'

'That's what I told the architect. Our sacred books, like the Vastu Shastra, tell us exactly how a temple has to be built, and we cannot change the layout. But he thinks Vitthala should have something that makes it different—something very unusual, that no temple has ever done before.' He shrugged. 'I don't really know what he means.'

Basava bent over the plan, the lamplight flickering and flaring over the thin lines and thought, *I could try and tell him what the temple looks like finished, but how do I do that?* Then he closed his eyes, trying to remember the Vitthala temple as it was in his time. He looked at the plan again and thought, *there is something missing here.* And then his heart missed a beat— he had got his answer.

He took a deep breath. *I have to say this very, very carefully,* he warned himself, *or he will get suspicious. As it is, Sivakka and I have said many odd things already.* Then he pointed tentatively to the plan, at an empty spot in the open courtyard right in front of the natya mandapam, and said, 'What will you have here? The courtyard looks too empty.'

'You can't have anything there. All pavilions and halls are already in place.'

'What about a chariot for Vitthala?' Basava said softly.

'You mean the wooden chariot-cars that all temples have? That chariot will stand outside on the road; because it has to be pulled down the road during the annual festival. We can't have it inside in the courtyard. Also how will we get a tall chariot car through the gopura gate?'

'No... no...I mean, suppose you had a small

stone chariot here.' Basava slid a quick glance towards Kartik to check how he was taking it. 'A ratha made of stone instead of wood, with carvings? Just to fill this space?' Then he sat quietly and waited for Kartik's imagination to take over; he couldn't possibly say more without giving himself away.

Kartik gave him a startled glance; then his face turned still and thoughtful. 'A ratha, a stone ratha?' He sat and brooded over the plan, and once in a while mumbled softly to himself, 'A ratha? With huge carved stone wheels...' He thought some more. 'With the top in brick for the figures...' He frowned. 'But who will ride the chariot?' Then he sat up, his eyes glittering with excitement. 'Of course! Garuda, the vahana of Lord Vitthala—he will ride it!' He waved at Basava. 'Get me some paper, I have to draw it now!' he said, pulling the pen and ink closer. Then he asked, 'What made you think of it, Basava? Do you dream of sculpture like I do? Sometimes I think you have a second sight or something.' Then he got so busy with his ideas, he completely forgot to think about Basava's oddness.

Ah, so he did design it, Basava thought with satisfaction. As he watched an absorbed Kartik working in the flickering light of the lamp, a rough drawing of the stone chariot-car of the Vitthala temple slowly appeared. *I did think that no one but Kartikeyan could have created something so beautiful.* Then he yawned—it had been a long day. It was past midnight when he left Kartik, still bent over his drawing; and when he wished him goodnight Kartik didn't even hear him.

Sivakka was still awake and waiting for him, and he remembered there was one more thing that he had to do. It was time to start planning to go home, and that meant he had to start carving the Ganesha. He pulled out the small piece of granite he had brought from the temple site, picked up the magic hammer and chisel, and said, 'Suppose we get back right now? You won't mind missing Padma's recital?'

But it was night, and little Siva was missing her amma. 'I want to go home! Please, please…'

'Fine. But stay close to me, hold on to my arm.'

With Sivakka clinging to him, he began to carve a dancing Ganesha. He placed the chisel on the stone, and with a small prayer to Vitthala he hit the chisel with the hammer and waited breathlessly. Nothing happened. They looked at each other, wide-eyed; then he bent to carve on.

Slowly, the shape of the figure appeared, the arms in a dancing pose, the curved legs. They looked around—they were still in Padma's house. After a while, he packed away the half-done figure saying, 'Siva, I'm too tired—I'll make a mistake. We'll try again tomorrow. I'm sure it'll work.'

Sivakka's eyes were wide with panic. 'Oh devaiyya! What if it doesn't and we never get home?'

Basava hugged her close. 'We will, Siva. We will.'

⚬⚭⚬

Next morning, as usual, Basava was shopping at the vegetable market in the lane behind the temple. The vegetable sellers sat with baskets of gourds and spinach, brinjals, lemons, chillies, radish, pumpkins... Basava wandered about, smelling the air and admiring the lovely colours of the fresh papayas, drumsticks and jackfruit. The air was full of the calls of the vegetable sellers, the spice merchants, the man with a basket of fish—that still flopped about—caught in the Tungabhadra. In the noise, he at first did not quite catch the whisper behind him.

Then someone said again, 'Boy, do you work for Padmalaya, the dancer?' Basava turned to see Ramaiyya, the mridangam player standing beside him. He nodded curtly and was turning away when Ramaiyya clutched his arm and said urgently, 'Please listen to me; I don't have much time. But will you tell her that Raghunath and Meenakshi are planning to ruin—'

'She knows about their plans. You are to let her down at the last minute.'

'I can't face her, I am so ashamed. Tell her I am going back to my village today and won't be back for some months. So she should find another player and begin rehearsing with him.'

'She's been looking, but everyone is scared of Raghunath...'

Ramaiyya, a small, middle-aged man with a lined, tired face, stood thoughtfully for a while. Then he said, 'Ask her to go to the houses by the tank on the other side of the Matanga hill, and ask for a drummer called Ponniah. He is my guru and one of the greatest mridangam players in this city. And he is not afraid of anyone. Also warn her, he is a little odd and will need to be persuaded. But if anyone can play at short notice and without making a mistake, it is Ponniah.'

Grabbing a few vegetables, Basava hurried home and reported everything to Padma and Kartik. Within minutes, the four of them were on their way, looking for Ponniah, the slightly mad mridangam player.

On one side of the Matanga hill was the main bazaar, and on the other was a small locality of thatched houses, where weavers and carpenters worked. It was here, in one corner, that they discovered the house of Ponniah. He was sitting in the courtyard, under a neem tree, repairing a mridangam. *He looks a bit mad too*, thought Sivakka.

Ponniah was an old man with snow-white hair flaring out around his head like a halo. He sat bare-chested, wearing a short dhoti. His lined face was thin, with hollow cheeks, the nose curving out imperiously, and when he looked up, they saw the large, deep-set, angry-looking eyes.

'What do you want?' he asked in a hoarse voice. 'I don't play anymore. So go away.'

Padma bowed low in a namaskar. 'I am Padmalaya. I dance at the Virupaksha temple.'

'I know that,' the old man said shortly. 'So

what? I don't play any more for silly flighty dancers.'

Padma swallowed nervously and went on, 'I have had the courage to come to you, Ponniah sir, only because your pupil Ramaiyya asked me to.' At hearing Ramaiyya's name the old man nodded. 'He said you are the greatest mridangam player in the kingdom and, sir, I need your help.'

'Why can't he play for you?'

Padma told him everything that had happened in the last few days, and the old man finally laid down the drum and listened. 'Ramaiyya is a good man but weak—you should never get bullied by a priest like Raghunath. I have heard of you. Ramaiyya says you are the best dancer in the temple, better than that fat one. He is scared of her too.' He laughed in a deep, husky growl, as if he smoked a lot of tobacco.

'But you are not afraid of anyone, are you?' Kartik asked shrewdly.

Ponniah laughed. 'No, I'm not. And you are a clever man to say so. Are you the Kartik, the one carving the yalis on the pillars at the Vitthala?' Kartik nodded. 'You are good, and you are not afraid either.' Kartik gave him a startled glance. 'You cannot be a good artist if you are afraid.' Then, he thought for a moment and, turning to Padma, he said, 'I'll play for you; we can't let that stupid priest win. We'll rehearse this evening.'

Padma's face bloomed with relief as she smiled. 'Will you come to my house?'

'Wait!' Sivakka said. 'If you rehearse there, Meenakshi could find out and then start planning something else. We have to do this in secret.'

'This girl is smart.' Ponniah grinned at Sivakka, showing a few missing teeth. 'Sharp as a chilli.' And Sivakka happily smiled back.

'The best place would be at the Vitthala,' Kartik said. 'Once the workmen leave, the place is deserted and there are no houses close by either.' He smiled gently at Padma. 'Come there with some lamps, and you can be the first dancer to dance in my natya mandapam.'

'Basava,' said Sivakka busily, 'we have to buy some lamps from the market. And Kartik Anna, we'll need some oil for the lamps.'

'Yes, Chilli Devi,' said Kartik obediently, and for the first time in days, Padma laughed.

It was evening and they were ready for rehearsal. The sun had dipped down behind the horizon, but the mellow light of the dying day still remained. All the carvers, masons, and labourers had left, and it was very quiet around the Vitthala temple, with just the calls of the birds returning to their nests. Ponniah sat with the singer who always sang for Padma. He was tapping and tuning his mridangam, while the singer held small metal cymbals to keep the beat. Sivakka and Basava had filled the natya mandapam with earthen lamps, and Kartik said it felt like Deepavali. The flames flared and flickered by the pillars. As the singer cleared his throat, Padma tucked her sari up, touched the feet of Ponniah and the singer, took a deep breath, and was ready to dance.

Today, Padma wore a simple white cotton sari—no glittering jewellery, no silks, no kohl around the eyes or reddened lips. But to Sivakka, she looked specially beautiful. She began with just quick, sharp movements—a sway of the arms, a tap of the feet, moving her eyes and brows, and then it got faster and faster as she, the drummer, and the singer kept perfect pace with each other. Then she began to dance to a padam, a beautiful song in worship of Lord Krishna, and her face and body moved in perfect, fluid grace as she played out the love story of Krishna and Satyabhama. Finally, she danced a slow, thoughtful song of devotion to the god, and Sivakka sat still in astonished joy. She didn't know anyone could dance like this. This was a Padmalaya she had never seen.

Sivakka thought of all the dancers she had seen—the ones who came to Hampi, Meenakshi, other dancers at the temple, the ones she had watched on the television in their village school—but this was different. As Padma's dancing figure moved between the pillars in the light and shadow of the lamps, she was not trying to dazzle her audience or win applause; she seemed to be dancing a prayer. She was the true devadasi, the handmaiden of the god, and she was offering up her life and soul to him. And even though the sanctum of the temple had no idol, it felt as if there was one, and it was Lord Vitthala himself who was watching her. When she finally came to the end of her recital, she stood quivering slightly, framed in the lamplight. Slowly, the singer brought his song to an end and there was a long silence in the temple.

Everyone was speechless, then Ponniah spoke gently, 'Devi Padmalaya, it is an honour, playing for you.'

Padma, still panting a bit, came and sat down beside Ponniah and said, 'I've never heard anyone play the mridangam like you. It was amazing. This was the first time you were playing with me and you did not miss a beat. How did you know every time what I was going to do next?'

Ponniah laughed. 'I can read minds and yours is very easy to read.' Then he laid his thin, veined hand on her head and said, 'Promise me, Padmalaya, you'll never stop dancing.'

It was late when they finished dinner. Padma had a quiet, dreamy look on her face all through, and Sivakka knew she was tired but happy. Now Meenakshi and Raghunath couldn't stop them. As Ponniah had said fiercely, Padma would dance even if he had to personally beat up Raghunath. And, Kartik and Basava had agreed to join him with great enthusiasm.

So, that night when they were in their room, and Basava picked up the half-done Ganesha,

Sivakka said apologetically, 'Actually Basava, do you think we could go back after Padma Akka's recital?'

Basava grinned. 'I thought you would say that! Wasn't she something? I kept thinking that if I could capture even a small bit of her beauty in a carving, it would be a miracle.'

'I do miss Amma and Appa,' Sivakka brooded, 'but to see her dance just one more time.'

'I'll start carving again the night after her recital,' Basava said. 'You know, I have been thinking. I think we'll travel ahead only once the carving is complete, because the Ganesha I had done in Hampi was nearly done when we travelled back to Vijayanagar. If only I could remember exactly what I was carving when it happened...'

'You're sure it will work?'

Basava gave her a quick doubtful look. 'How can I be sure? I've never done it before.'

It will work. I'm sure it will, prayed Sivakka to herself.

chapter seven

It was the day of Padmalaya's recital at the Krishna temple. Sivakka, who now considered herself Padma's assistant, got up early to make sure everything was ready. She and Padma got busy laying out the costume, checking her make-up boxes, selecting the jewellery. Sivakka rushed off to Manjira to make sure she would have the garlands ready on time. Padma would need a long one for her hair. Then, midmorning, Kartik arrived and said to the children, 'Let's go.'

Padma gave him a startled look, 'Where to? It's too early.'

'No, no, not to the temple. I'm taking you all to the palace. There is a special parade to celebrate our victory at Raichur, and I've managed to get invitations for all of us.'

Padma shook her head. 'I'm not going

anywhere today. I don't want to get tired. Take the children with you.'

So Kartik, Basava and Sivakka took a bullock cart to the palace area of Vijayanagar. The last time they had come, was when Padma was to dance for the queen. This time, instead of going towards the queen's zenana, they turned right to the area where the palaces of the king and the royal princes and nobles stood. They walked past the Hazara Rama temple and turned into the main palace enclosure.

Basava looked around, and then stood still in wonder, saying softly, 'Kartik Anna, is this heaven or are we still on earth?'

Kartik laughed. 'The place where Krishnadeva Raya lives has to be special.'

Stretching before them, as far as the eye could see, were the most magnificent palaces, pavilions, watchtowers, orchards, gardens, and snaking through it all, the raised stone channel of the aqueduct that brought water from the Tungabhadra river. Sivakka commented that it was also much cleaner than the temple area—there were no open drains or garbage dumps, no cows and goats wandering about, no beggars or calling vendors. Kartik pointed out the different palaces. In front of them was the king's audience hall. Next to it was the tallest building in the area—a huge palace on a high, many-storeyed carved base, called the Mahanavami Dibba. This was where the king performed religious ceremonies, and stood to take the salute from his soldiers during the mahanavami celebrations at Dussehra every year.

Beyond that were many smaller palaces, where the royal family and important noblemen lived. They walked closer to the aqueduct and saw a beautiful square pool into which the water was pouring in. It was made with an unusual green stone and the design was very different from all the other buildings—there were no carvings, just straight-cut steps in an intricate geometric design going down to the water edge. Basava remembered that the government people had discovered this pool buried under the ground, and had dug it up. However, in their Hampi, there was no water in the aqueduct, so the pool was dry.

They found space to sit in front of the Mahanavami Dibba to watch the parade, and Basava looked up at the huge palace looming up before him. In their Hampi, all that was left was the high, three-storeyed stone base, with the rows and rows of carvings of marching soldiers, horses, elephants and, surprisingly, camels. The actual palace had, however, vanished, and now he knew why—it was made of wood and brick, and not stone. The tall wooden pillars were carved and inlaid in silver and ivory, with colourful canopies draped between them. Flags flew on top of the brick roof and he could see the rich carpets laid out on the steps. When the invaders from Bijapur and Golconda came, they must have looted the precious things and then set fire to the palace, burning the wooden walls and pillars so that only the stone base had survived.

Basava thought how in the evenings he and his friends often played on the stone platform of the Mahanavami Dibba. He turned to Kartik. 'This must be the highest spot in the city—won't it be great to sit on top and watch the sunset?'

Kartik grinned. 'Sure. We'll go up to the king and say, "Sir, can we watch the sunset from your bedroom? We hear it's a grand sight."' He lightly slapped a grinning Basava on the head. 'You want me to lose my head?'

Basava and Sivakka shared a secret smile. In their Hampi, they often sat on the Dibba, watching the sun dip down below the horizon, and Sivakka and her friends liked to dance the hit numbers from films on the high platform— just for fun. It was one of their favourite places, and they had never imagined that a great king had once lived there.

Sivakka, who was looking down the road, suddenly said, 'Help! Here comes trouble.' And then said warningly, 'Be very careful, please, everyone.'

They turned to see Meenakshi and her maid walking towards them. The moment she saw Kartik, she gave a huge smile, as if he was one of her dearest friends, and said, 'What a pleasant surprise to see you here, Kartikeyan! And the sweet children too! My dear Padmalaya hasn't come with you?'

Kartik's smile was just as wide and as false. 'She did not want to tire herself before the recital tonight.'

'Of course! I quite understand. I hope her rehearsals have gone smoothly. Has Ramaiyya been playing well?'

Kartik nodded. 'Ramaiyya is excellent, as usual.'

Then, as the three of them sat with smiles pasted on their faces, Meenakshi swept past them, and they heard her say something to the maid, and the two women laughed.

'Sweet children! My dear Padmalaya!' Sivakka mimicked her. 'Last time she called me a spy. Oh, won't it be fun when she sees Padma Akka dance before the king?'

The stands for the common people were already jammed, when in the palace before them, the noble and powerful people of Vijayanagar began to arrive. Basava noticed that it was Saluva Timma who was receiving all the guests. Then, two tall and very fair men, wearing odd clothes, arrived. They wore tight trousers, shirts with huge sleeves, high-heeled shoes, and large hats.

'Who are they?' he asked Kartik. 'I've seen others like them in the bazaar.'

'They come from a place on the west coast called Goa, but actually their real home is a far-off kingdom across the seas. They travel for months by ships bringing very good Arab horses that the king buys for the army.'

Basava remembered something he had read in school. 'They come from a kingdom called Portugal.'

Kartik shrugged, 'Must be. Vijayanagar is the richest kingdom in the land, so these traders come from all across the world. The Arabs come to buy our cotton and silks, the Chinese bring silks, jade and paper; and these pale-faced men sell us horses and fill their ships with our spices.'

More guests were arriving. The nayakas, or governors of the provinces, came wearing huge, proud turbans. The queens came to sit behind a carved wooden screen. Kartik pointed out the famous poet Allasani Pedana, who was standing beside Tenali Rama. Both men were busy helping Timma with the guests.

Then the ceremony began. From one end, the temple dancers—the devadasis—trooped in, shimmering in silks and glittering with jewels, and began to dance, making Sivakka sigh in delight. Then the royal horses and elephants were led in. The horses, stamping and snorting, were all covered with rich cloths, while behind them stood a row of swaying elephants, painted and draped in silks. On the dais, a young man was ceremoniously led to a seat by the king's throne, and Kartik told them he was Kumara Virya, the prince of the kingdom of Seringapatam and Queen Tirumale Devi's brother.

Finally, the king arrived. Today, Krishnadeva Raya was dressed for a royal celebration. He wore a dhoti in white silk—covered with rich gold embroidery—which flowed to his ankles, and carried a silk brocade shawl across his shoulders. He was bare-chested, but covered in jewellery. Pearls and diamonds glittered in the necklace around his neck, and on the armlets and bracelets on his arms. On his head he wore a tall, embroidered gold brocade crown. He came walking below the dais, followed by a priest carrying flowers and a lamp on a puja salver.

The king walked up to the royal horses and elephants, and as the priest chanted mantras, he threw flowers at the animals and worshipped them. Then he walked up the steps to the top of the Mahanavami Dibba and, standing before his throne, he raised his hands with a wide smile to acknowledge the loud cheers from the crowd. His throne was a flat seat made of gold, with many precious stones set on it. It was covered with silks and had large bolsters for him to lean on. Two women stood behind, fanning him with huge, decorated peacock-feather fans. Then the king waved to the soldiers and the parade began.

First, all the soldiers who had fought bravely at the battle for Raichur were rewarded. One by one, captains of the infantry, archers, cavalrymen, and musketeers walked up the step to receive bags of coins. Some of the bravest soldiers bowed, as their king put gold chains around their necks. Then the triumphant Vijayanagar army came marching. First, horses carried the standard of the king—flaring royal flags, and silver and gold emblems. Then the infantry swept past—rows and rows of foot soldiers carrying swords and shields. The cavalry rode by on horses, their spears—adorned with high-flying flags—glinting in the sun. Each rider wore a short sword and dagger at his belt. The archers carried their bows and arrows, and the musketeers, with their cannons, followed them. All the while, the drummers and flute players played, and the devadasis danced. It was really a grand sight.

That evening, Padmalaya was getting ready for the most important recital of her life. Sivakka and Manjira had helped her put on the sari that the queen had sent her, then plaited her long hair and decorated it with jasmines. She had made up her eyes with kohl and reddened her lips with lac. Now, for the final touch, Sivakka opened the box of jewellery.

First, the two small brooches shaped like the sun and moon went on her hair, and the netti chutti—the gold thread—in the parting. She put on a nose-ring set with pearls, and in her ears she wore thodus—small gold ear tops. The crocodile-shaped vankhi armlets snaked up her forearms. Then she put on the pearl bangles, and around her neck she wore the manga malai—the gold necklace with pendants of mango motifs in rubies and diamonds—the queen had sent her. She wrapped the gold belt with bells, called the mekhala, across her hips. Sivakka was to carry her heavy, belled anklets— she would put them on just before the recital.

Kartik came in wearing his best clothes and looking surprisingly neat, with his hair combed, dhoti smartly pleated, and carrying a cloth packet that he handed to Sivakka. Opening the packet, an excited Sivakka discovered a set of new clothes for her and Basava. A pink blouse and a long skirt for her, and a blue tunic and white dhoti for Basava. Manjira also wore a bright blue sari, and had even bought a gold necklace just for the occasion. As she said, how many times can a garland girl sit in the same place as the king? They all looked very pleased with themselves, feeling rather magnificent, but then Malappa arrived, and they gasped in astonishment at the sight.

Instead of his short dhoti and tatty tunic, today he wore a cream and gold-bordered dhoti that flowed to his ankles in elegant folds. On top, he wore a long-sleeved tunic with gold buttons, and on his head he had a fantastic turban with a fan-shaped knot that had added inches to his height. He even smelled of an expensive perfume, and in one hand he carried a long-stemmed rose which he ceremoniously presented to Padma with a low bow. Everyone was quite speechless, though Basava thought, amused, his crooked grin was the same.

'What do you think?' he posed with a casual air, and asked with a superior smile.

'I can't believe it!' Manjira's eyes were round

with wonder. 'Where did you find these clothes and those gold buttons?'

'They are not stolen, if you are worried about that. And if you marry me, I will look even grander. I have just ordered a long gold chain at my jeweller's.'

⌘

An hour later, they were at the Krishna temple. The puja to enshrine the idol had been completed by a group of priests the day before— it was an image of Balakrishna that the king had brought from a temple in Udayagiri. All the guests were seated around the pillared hall before the sanctum of the idol. Sivakka and the others were seated right behind the musicians. Basava wondered in amusement what the royal guests would do if they knew that the solemn, turbaned gentleman sitting beside him was once the smartest burglar in town. As if reading his thoughts, Malappa gave a regal smile.

From where she sat, Sivakka could see Meenakshi and Raghunath, and she kept her eyes on them all the time. This was something she wasn't going to miss for anything in the world. At first, the fat dancer was looking very pleased with herself, happily chewing paan and chatting with Raghunath. Then she noticed how calmly all Padma's friends were sitting, and she looked a bit puzzled. She obviously expected them to be running around looking for a drummer. Finally, when the musicians trooped in, her mouth fell open at the sight of Ponniah and his mridangam. And today, the old drummer was also looking really impressive, with his snowy hair neatly combed like a halo around his head. Meenakshi turned to mutter furiously at Raghunath, and Sivakka saw him shrug. Meenakshi's face was red with fury as she and Raghunath sat and glared at Ponniah, who calmly glared back. As he had told them, he wasn't afraid of anyone.

To the soft call of the flute, Padmalaya slowly entered and stood still for a moment, facing her audience before turning to do an elaborate pranaam to the idol. She danced exactly what she had rehearsed with Ponniah that evening at the Vitthala temple, but this time there was a glittering, majestic flair to it all. *She really does look like an apsara*, Sivakka thought, enchanted. By the light of the tall, many-flamed brass lamps that filled the temple with a golden glow, she swirled and swayed in and out between the pillars like a shimmering butterfly, as Ponniah shook his head and his tapping fingers kept perfect beat with her flying feet. From where they sat, they couldn't see the royal guests, but they could hear their murmurs of approval. *She is fabulous as always*, thought Sivakka, *but that night at the Vitthala, she was not trying to dazzle anyone—it was just Padma dancing to her god.* For Sivakka, that dance at Vitthala was special.

After the first few minutes of watching Padma, Basava's mind, as usual, began to wander. He looked around, studying all the sculptures on the pillars, and then he began to worry about something he had buried at the back of his mind till now. It was time to return to Hampi, and he hadn't a clue how to go back. He was just guessing wildly when he told Sivakka that it could be done by carving a dancing Ganesha. He had said that only to reassure her, but he had no idea if it would work. And worse, there was the fear that they may end up somewhere else in the past. *Oh devaiyya*, he thought desperately, *if we can't go home then let us stay on with Padma in Vijayanagar; I can't bear to think of landing in some other time.*

He took a deep breath, trying hard to calm his nerves and remember very carefully, minute by minute, what he had done that last afternoon in Hampi. He closed his eyes and let his mind travel back: they had settled down on the Kodandarama road; he had pulled out the half-done Ganesha, and the magic hammer and chisel. Sivakka was leaning against his shoulders, chattering away; he was talking about King Krishnadeva Raya's Vijayanagar as he finished the eyebrows, then...Yes! Now he knew! He began carving the eyes! So he had to carve the eyes of the Ganesha, with Sivakka sitting close to him and...Of course! He had to talk about the place where he wanted to travel. *Oh please, I hope I've got it right,* he prayed to his favourite god, Lord Virupaksha. *Please let Sivakka and me go home. This is your servant Basava, and I promise you a puja of laddu, murukku, and bananas.*

Late that night, Sivakka and Basava stood at the door of Padma's house, watching Manjira, Malappa, and Kartik going home. Watching Kartikeyan's receding back vanishing down the lane, there was a lump in Basava's throat as he thought, *Kartik will never know how special he is to me: he has become my guru, who taught me that I can do what I dream of doing.*

Then, a tired and deliriously happy Padma finally went to bed. The king had sent a message that he had liked her performance, and Queen Tirumale Devi was very pleased. Padma was to be the Chief Dancer of the Krishna temple, with a house and an allowance. When Sivakka and Basava hugged her goodnight, she happily hugged them back. In the lamplight she did not see the tears shimmering in their eyes. They did want to go home, but neither of them had imagined how hard it would be to say goodbye to these kind and gentle people.

Finally, Basava picked up the magic chisel and hammer, and put the half-done figure of the dancing Ganesha on his lap. He turned and made sure Sivakka was leaning against him, and began to carve. But this time they were sad and silent as he finished carving the eyebrows. Then, with a small prayer, as he began carving the eyes, Basava began to repeat softly under his breath, 'Amma...Appa...Hampi... Karnataka...India...'

Just as he finished carving the second eye, once again their heads began to spin faster and faster. There was the sound of thunder in their ears; everything was swaying wildly, and there were starry lights behind their eyes. Basava and Sivakka clutched on to each other, and just before everything went dark, Basava's last thoughts were, *It works! I guessed right! We are travelling in time, but are we going to get back to our Hampi?*

chapter eight

Slowly their heads stopped spinning, and they opened their eyes and looked around nervously Where were they? This wasn't the road to the Kodandarama temple! This was a rice field! Oh no! They exchanged a panicked glance. They were lost again! And then, as they looked around, the panic slowly lessened as they calmed down, and things got straightened up in their minds.

The place looked very familiar; it felt like home—and they realized they really were in their own village of Hampi, just at another spot. As Basava worked it out, they were at the place where Padma's house must have stood in ancient Vijayanagar. They were standing at one corner of the field that now ran through the broken-down bazaar that faced the ruined Krishna temple. He looked down and realized he was still holding the magic hammer and chisel.

'You stay at the same spot where you were when the magic starts,' he explained to his sister, 'and this time we were not on the hill road but inside Padma Akka's house. Look, our clothes are the ones we were wearing at Hampi.'

Sivakka, however, didn't look completely convinced. Were they in the Hampi of their own time or not?

They climbed up to the main road and began walking towards home. Taking the shortcut through the fields past the Narasimha statue, slowly Sivakka began to smile. Yes, this was all very familiar. There was the old man who acted as a guide, sitting near the statue, smoking. Beyond that she could see the soft drinks stall of Suresh, who lived in their village; and who was that running towards them through the banana grove?

'Venkataaaa!' they yelled, waving and jumping about in delight. Oh! What a relief! They really were home!

Venkata ran up to them with his usual wide grin and said, 'Oye, what's the excitement? Found some treasures or what?' and then nearly tumbled to the ground as Basava and Sivakka jumped on him, hugging him hard. 'What's up? Let me go! You two gone mad or something?'

They moved back, a bit embarrassed, as Basava asked, 'Didn't you miss us when we were away? We missed you.'

'Away? Where did you go and when? I was with you this morning when we repaired the pillar at the pavilion and then we went home for lunch.'

'This morning!'

'Of course! And it was last night that we sneaked up to the bazaar roof and saw the dancer.' Venkata frowned at them. 'You two are okay? Not sick or anything, are you?'

Basava and Sivakka stared at each other as it slowly dawned on them that, while they had been at Vijayanagar, with so much happening, time hadn't passed at all in Hampi! They had come back to the same day and the same time.

Basava grinned weakly, trying hard to cover up. 'Well, it was nearly six hours ago; it's evening now. You should have missed us…' he ended a bit lamely.

Venkata shrugged. 'Miss you after six hours? I won't miss you for six days! I always knew you two are a bit crazy. You know, some of the screws in your heads move backwards.'

Just then Sivakka gave a small jump and said, 'Oh, help! My coconuts! They are still lying on the road. I forgot to pack them, and your bag of carvings is also there. We'd better go back now.'

'No one will steal your coconuts,' Basava said. 'I'll just pop in at home to see Amma, and then I'll go back to pack things up.' He picked up the hammer and chisel that he had dropped in his excitement at seeing Venkata. 'Come on, Siva. I want to go home!'

Venkata jumped up to reach a hanging bunch of bananas and, helping himself to one, said, 'I'll see you two later. Right now, I have to meet Viru at the cycle repair shop.' With a wave, he wandered off down the road. Basava gave a small sigh of relief—at least Venkata hadn't taken their crazy behaviour too seriously.

As they walked home, they worked it out. No one would have missed them in Hampi, and in a way that was a relief. It meant their parents wouldn't have worried and gone around searching for their lost children!

'But does that mean they have forgotten about us in Vijayanagar too?' Sivakka mused.

'You mean Padma Akka and Kartik Anna don't even remember that we were there with them for all these days?'

'Probably. But then, look at the bright side: they won't look for us, and Padma Akka won't miss us and feel sad. I had hated the idea of her searching for us.'

'But does that mean all that happened to us never took place? Malappa and you hiding in the temples, Padma Akka dancing, the fight with Meenakshi...'

'I don't know...'Basava brooded. 'Maybe it all happened; just that we weren't there. This magic somehow made us a part of it, like entering a play...' He then added thoughtfully, 'But the carvings are there still, so is the stone chariot; and Krishnadeva Raya did install a Balakrishna idol at the temple...' His face brightened. 'Well, we could always go back again to check—now that I know how the magic works! And we could take Venkata, Ratna, Radha and Viru with us!'

'Not for a while, thank you,' Sivakka said firmly. 'There are exams coming and then there is the family wedding next month...' Her smile widened at an idea. 'At the wedding, I could dance something that Padma Akka taught me!'

'I don't know about you, but I will go back. My lessons with Kartikeyan are not over. If I can learn some more, then when I begin work with the government people, I could show them how well I can carve. And they may even let me do some of the repairs on the carvings. And can you imagine, Siva, I know how these buildings looked like when they were new! I can describe them and help restore them correctly, though I will have to be very careful how I say it.'

Then Sivakka asked the question that had occurred to him too. 'Basava, does this mean we can't talk about our adventures to anyone? I'm dying to tell everyone about it.'

'They won't believe us. They'll think we made it all up and laugh. Appa could even get angry. After all, we haven't been missing at all. They'll all ask how could we spend so many days in another place in the past while time didn't pass at all at Hampi? I don't have any answers. Do you?'

'But I have to tell someone! I have to tell Amma and Appa, if no one else,' Sivakka said stubbornly. 'Or it will all rumble away inside me and give me a headache.'

'Tell them tomorrow. Just say that you had

this dream.' Basava smiled slightly. 'It already seems like a dream.'

By then they had reached home. They saw their mother sitting on the porch of their house, repairing one of Sivakka's school skirts. She smiled as they sat down on each side of her, and looked a little puzzled at the huge smiles and sudden flurry of hugs from her children. She asked a bit suspiciously, like all mothers do, 'What's up? You two must be very hungry to hug me like that.'

'Yes, Amma.' Sivakka squeezed her arm tight in delight. 'I thought you were going to make potato bajjis for us.' And across their mother's bent head, they grinned at each other. They were truly home at last.

❧

Later in the evening, leaving Sivakka still clinging to her mother and chattering away, Basava walked through the Hampi bazaar to the hill road that led to the Kodandarama temple. His mind was a jumble of images and memories. He compared the ruined bazaar— the hippies lying around in the arcades, the cheap little shops selling trinkets, the garish restaurants serving coffee and sandwiches—and thought of how beautiful it all had been once. He looked up to the tall spire of the gopura of the Virupaksha temple and thought, *I saw Padmalaya dance there.* The corner arcade which had once been Manjira's garland shop was now a dirty little cafe, with a man in a lungi serving up idlis on plastic plates. Basava sighed with sadness.

All their things—coconuts and carvings—were lying exactly where they had left them. As he gathered them, suddenly, he thought of the two women from Delhi who had bought his carvings. One of them had picked a dancing Ganesha. *What would she have thought about our adventures,* he wondered. She did look the kind who wouldn't have laughed at the story. He packed up the coconuts and the carvings in gunny sacks, and left them at the back of a nearby tea shop where the man let them store the things for the night. Then he walked on towards the Vitthala temple. He hadn't really said a proper goodbye to Chinappa and Kartikeyan yet.

It was a long walk by the riverbank, and dusk was falling when he reached the Vitthala temple. He wandered in and walked into the ruined natya mandapam, and suddenly it was as if Padmalaya was still dancing there, as Ponniah shook his mane of hair and played the mridangam. He sat under the gorgeous carved ceiling of the kalyana mandapam and watched the last of the day's visitors slowly drifting out of the temple. The tourist guides were collecting their charges and heading for the buses. There were no men bent over slabs of granite, no sound of hammers hitting chisel, no Chinappa lecturing him about the right way to carve a lotus flower or the way to curve the hand of an apsara.

Then he suddenly thought, *I forgot to tell Tenali Rama that his clown was ready and he could take it home. If it's there of course*, he brooded. *Maybe all the carvings I did vanished too.* He walked about studying the pillars thinking, *this is Chinappa's apsara, that is Kartik's yali.* He smiled to himself as he walked across the courtyard, past the stone chariot with its huge wheels that Kartik was still designing when they left. Then, standing in the bhajana mandapam he bent to look at the panels on a pillar and his heart stood still.

There it was: the bottom panel on the corner pillar, the funny-looking man in a belled cap, holding a rattle, his legs bent comically at the knees—his clown, Tenali's royal jester. Time had faded the carving a bit but it was still Malappa's face.

Chinappa must have carved this like he was planning to, copying my design, Basava's heart sang. *So I have left something in Vijayanagar*, he thought, his mind flooding with joy. *This clown is mine, and it is here in the Vitthala temple. I, Basava, a poor farmer's son in the village of Hampi in the twenty-first century, I am also a royal sculptor of King Krishnadeva Raya of Vijayanagar.*

historical note
the story of vijayanagar–hampi

In the fourteenth century, when Sultan Muhammad bin Tughlak was ruling in Delhi, a new kingdom rose in south India—the kingdom of Vijayanagar. Two brothers, Harihar and Bukka—local chieftains in the region that is modern Karnataka—were captured by the forces of the sultan and taken to Delhi. Here, they were forced to convert to Islam and then sent back to the south as governors.

Returning home, the brothers met their guru, the sage Vidyaranya, gave up Islam, and established their own kingdom by the banks of the Tungabhadra river. In AD 1336, Harihar became the king of the new kingdom of Hampi-Hastinavati, and they began building their capital city called Vijayanagar. Later, the kingdom came to be called after the city.

In the fifteenth and sixteenth centuries, Vijayanagar was one of the most fabulous cities in the world, rivalling even London and Delhi. Many travellers and traders from Europe came here, and some of the best descriptions of the city and its people can be found in the writings of two Portuguese travelers, Domingo Paes and Fernao Nuniz.

Vijayanagar was often at war with the other kingdoms in the south like the Bahmanis and later the kingdoms of Bijapur, Golconda and Odisha. The kings followed a policy of religious tolerance, and the army had many Muslims soldiers. King Deva Raya II even had a mosque built for them.

The greatest king of Vijayanagar was Krishnadeva Raya who ruled from AD 1509 to AD 1529. By then the kingdom covered most of the southern peninsula, including most of present-day Tamil Nadu, Kerala, and Karnataka. In his glittering court was a courtier and humourist named Tenali Rama. A poem written by Krishnadeva Raya has survived, and so have the funny stories of the exploits of

Tenali. Basava and Sivakka travel back in time to this period of Vijayanagar's history.

The city of Vijayanagar was at its zenith at that time. It was filled with busy bazaars, beautiful palaces and temples. Sculpture and painting, dance and music, literature and philosophy were all encouraged by the king. Some of the most beautiful palaces and temples—including the Krishna temple where Padmalaya dances, and the Vitthala temple where Kartikeyan is working—were built by Krishnadeva Raya.

After Krishnadeva Raya a number of weak kings followed, and the empire began to decline. In 1565, a combined army of Bijapur and Golconda defeated Vijayanagar at the battle of Talikota. The invading army occupied the city and took a terrible revenge for years of defeat. Thousands were massacred, the palaces and temples were set on fire, the sculptures smashed.

Vijayanagar was abandoned by its people and never rose again. For centuries the ruins lay silent around the small village of Hampi. The greatness of Vijayanagar was forgotten till 1900 CE when Robert Sewell discovered the magnificent ruins and wrote about them.

Today, barring the Virupaksha temple and the ancient Hampi Bazaar, most of Vijayanagar is just ruins lying across the landscape. There is the small village of Hampi and, nearby, the town of Hospet where the tourists come to stay. The ruins are everywhere—pavilions in the middle of green rice fields, palaces by banana groves, pillars holding up the roofs of houses. And every inch of these ruins is embellished with magnificent carvings.

Some of the best carvings can be seen on the walls, pillars, and ceilings of the Vitthala temple. And on some of the pillars, among the figures of gods and goddesses, dancers and musicians, animals and flowers are figures of dancing jesters wearing a peaked cap. Padmalaya, Kartikeyan, Basava and Sivakka may be imaginary people, but the clown really does exist. Maybe it was carved to make Tenali Rama smile.